D1245361

QUINN

THE SHORT STORIES - VOLUME 1

KEVIN SCOTT OLSON

SOUTH POINTE PRESS

Quinn: The Short Stories - Volume 1

First Edition

Ebook ISBN: 978-1-7324172-7-4

Print ISBN: 978-1-7324172-6-7

Edited and formatted by Ben Wolf

www.benwolf.com

Cover design by Book Covers Art

www.bookcoversart.com

Available in print and ebook format on amazon.com.

**Reviews for the international bestseller
Michael Quinn novel *Night of the Bonfire*:**

"Five stars, worthy of ten… grabs your attention and takes you for a wild ride!" - Goodreads review

"Loaded with action… Michael Quinn is ready for his own series." - Kirkus review

"Had me holding my breath and tensing with suspense… can't wait for more." - Amazon review

"A master writer… couldn't put down the book until I finished." - Amazon review

FOR MORE WORKS BY THE AUTHOR, VISIT
WWW.KEVINSCOTTOLSON.COM

To Ben,
Ye of infinite patience

Once is happenstance. Twice is coincidence. Three times is enemy action.

— IAN FLEMING

CONTENTS

PARADISE

A MICHAEL QUINN SHORT STORY

KEVIN SCOTT OLSON

All limits had been passed.

— ELIE WIESEL

PARADISE

Evening
The Central California Coast

IN THE DARKNESS, IN THE RAGING STORM, THE BIG eighteen-wheeler rounded the curve too fast.

Michael Quinn slowed his motorcycle as the truck's headlights appeared around the bend in front of him.

It looked bad. The desolate stretch of Pacific Coast Highway, with the sea on one side and rolling hills on the other, left the rig fully exposed to the elements. Waves of rain slammed the asphalt and rippled under the tires, turning the truck into a speeding forty-ton hockey puck.

The truck's black cab slid over the centerline, out of control. The cab turned back but the trailer jackknifed, dragging the entire vehicle across both lanes.

Quinn's heart pounded his ears as he pulled over to the guardrail at the seaward edge of the two-lane highway. He wiped the rain off his goggles and did the quick mental math of survival.

The truck was less than fifty yards away and headed right at him. He had three, maybe four seconds before it struck him broadside. The semi blocked the highway, and there was no time, on this flooded road, for the careful maneuvering required to turn the bike around.

To his right, past the guardrail, the cliff dropped straight to the sea. To his left, darkness hid what lay beyond the other side of the highway. If he shot across the road he might drive up a nice, easy slope. Or he might slam into the earthen equivalent of a brick wall.

Panic swelled in his gut as the mass of black metal loomed in front of him. For a split-second, he considered ditching his bike and leaping over the guardrail. But now there was no time even for that—the bike's headlight shone off the truck's glossy hood.

He turned his headlight to shine on the gap between the guardrail and the speeding truck. It was maybe two feet wide. But it was a chance.

The truck's horn blasted like a train and the rig was almost on top of him. The driver's startled face flashed pasty white through the windshield. The man was shouting something, his hands yanking the steering wheel.

Now. Quinn gunned the throttle.

The bike rocketed forward into the gap. The rear tire skidded, then held. Quinn's boot scraped the guardrail and the bike wobbled as he shot past a blur of rain and wet metal.

Then the open road lay in front of him and he was

through. He swerved to a stop in the center of the highway and looked behind him.

Truck tires screeched and regained traction as the cab, inches from the guardrail, swung back toward the road. The trailer lurched sideways towards the sea, then straightened out and followed the cab to the safety of the inside lane.

The truck rounded a turn and vanished into the night. Pacific Coast Highway was once again a curving ribbon of darkness. The dull roar of the storm sounded in his ears.

For a moment Quinn sat there in the rain, catching his breath. Then he turned his bike back toward the open road and cruised slowly in the middle of the outside lane. His limbs shook from the near-death experience. Fistfuls of rain pelted him, and the handlebars twisted in the buffeting winds.

What had been so urgent that the driver chose to risk his life in this treacherous storm?

Perhaps the driver was behind schedule and worried about losing his job. Or amped on opioids. Maybe he was anxious to get to a date, to a woman impatiently waiting for him at a truck stop.

Quinn clenched his jaw as a gust of rain slammed his cheek. Those few seconds had almost been the end. Not in a blaze of glory. Not at the peaceful end of a long and fulfilling life. Random, aimless fate had come close to wrapping things up with an obscure highway accident, of interest only to the back pages of the local throwaway newspaper.

He passed a closed gas station, its old-fashioned circular pumps silhouetted in the darkness. This was a lone stretch of highway, without towns or streetlamps, nothing but finicky

3

Mother Nature in a bad mood. It would be a cold and miserable three-hour ride home.

The bike droned through a series of S-curves, then something glimmered ahead. Turquoise light, flashing off and on, floating as if some ethereal specter. Probably the light bar of a California Highway Patrol car. The CHP car might have stopped next to an accident.

The glimmer vanished as he rounded a curve into a stretch of road so pitch-black he felt the queasiness of vertigo.

Another bend and the turquoise light reappeared, this time larger and hovering in the air to his left. It wasn't a CHP car. He wiped his goggles, and the blurry light cleared into a twenty-foot tall neon sign.

The top line flashed *Paradise* in turquoise script with a neon palm tree above the word. The white block letters below read *Motor Court* and below that *Visit the Paradise Lounge*.

He slowed and looked behind the flashing sign. Queen Palm trees fronted the property, their tall trunks bent in submission to the storm. Behind them the motel office and its attached Paradise Lounge were unpretentious, single-story buildings facing the highway. Lights beckoned from the Lounge.

Anything that got him out of the rain sounded promising. His leather jacket kept his upper body dry, but his jeans were soaked through. He'd packed a change of clothes and his shaving kit in his duffel bag. The storm would pass during the night, and he could cruise home in the morning sunshine.

Not to mention the fact he'd almost been splattered across the highway.

One does not tempt fate twice in the same night.

He pulled over under the arched stucco portico and killed the engine. His tired legs ached as he climbed off the bike.

Twenty minutes later
The Paradise Lounge

A HOT SHOWER, A CHANGE OF CLOTHES, AND AN ICE-cold Negra Modelo made the world a friendlier place.

Quinn sat alone at the bar, his hand wrapped around the frosted bottle. He relaxed in his clean tee-shirt and jeans while the dark lager dissolved the road tension. On the muted television behind the bar, a pretty weather girl pointed to videos of mudslides and stranded motorists.

The décor of the Paradise Lounge stepped back decades in time. Knotty pine walls surrounded a well-preserved pool table and a dining area with wood tables and a handful of customers. Warmly lit with comfortable leather chairs, the humble room was a refuge from the rain pounding the roof and sheeting off the covered walkway.

The gray-haired, seventyish woman who'd served him lingered at the sink, washing glasses. She glanced at him.

"Can I get you anything else? Our kitchen is closed, but we have roast beef sandwiches."

"I'm fine, thank you, ma'am." Quinn sensed that she was the owner. He thought of the fifties-style décor and the old-fashioned coffeemaker and television console in his room. "Nice place you have here. Kind of a retro look?"

Her watery eyes shone with interest. "My guests have been

5

using that word for some time now. My husband and I inherited this place from my parents, back in the seventies. We were newlyweds."

She set down the glass she'd been drying and picked up another. "He passed a couple of years later—cancer—and all of a sudden I was a widow in my twenties. Decided to keep everything as it was. There used to be other motor courts along this stretch of highway, one with a giant neon cowboy sign, another with a big wigwam. Now I'm the only one left."

What caused the curious tendency of some people to pour out their life stories to traveling strangers? He was about to reply when a chair scraped behind him.

"Checkmate!" pinged a youthful female voice.

He swiveled on his barstool. A young woman sat at a table for two with a chess board in front of her. She wore jeans and a Stanford sweatshirt. An elderly white-haired man dressed in rumpled slacks and shirt, and a well-worn brown sport coat, sat across from her.

"Professor, you can't play chess and work on your memoirs at the same time." The young woman looked up from her game and folded her arms in mock impatience. Her hair was tucked up in a visor. The visor tilted up, and Quinn glimpsed honey-brown eyes.

"I am quite capable of multi-tasking." The man glanced at the chessboard, then went back to writing on a yellow legal pad. "And your play was so slow I decided to let you win this one. Memoirs must be completed during one's lifetime."

Something about the man was familiar.

Quinn realized he was staring and glanced around the room. The only other customers were two elderly couples having dessert and, in a booth on the far side, four men in coveralls talking quietly over bottles of beer.

"You have plenty of time, professor." The girl put the chess pieces back, then stood. She stretched, looked around the room, wandered over to the pool table, and selected a cue from the rack.

"I'm bored. Do you know how to play this game?" Her fingers caressed the cue tip. She was petite, inches taller than the cue. The baggy sweatshirt and lack of makeup indicated the sort of busy college student not overly concerned about her appearance.

"I know a great deal about history, a fair amount about chess, but nothing about that particular endeavor." The man picked up his whiskey and turned his gaze to Quinn. "Perhaps this young man would be kind enough to show you."

That voice, the refined use of English.

"It would be my pleasure, Dr. Hartman." Quinn eased off his barstool.

"We have met?" White eyebrows arched in puzzlement.

Quinn walked over to the table. "Several years ago. You were a visiting professor when I was a graduate student at Oxford. Your class 'Freedom in the Twenty-First Century' was quite memorable. Michael Quinn, sir."

The professor rose to shake his hand. "Forgive me, I— wait. Yes. I remember you from the after-class sessions at that coffee house." A warm smile creased his face. "Please, have a seat."

Across the room, the girl rolled the cue ball down the middle of the pool table. Quinn felt her watching him.

Time had deepened the lines on his face and freckled it

with age spots, but otherwise Dr. Hartman looked as Quinn remembered him. The angular features formed a kindly face. The lean torso showed little of the gravity-induced sagging that came with advanced age, and the snow-white hair revealed no signs of thinning.

Everything about Dr. Hartman's demeanor bespoke the civility of an Old-World academic. He sat in his chair in the patient manner he had in the coffee house discussion groups. When Quinn first saw him lecture at Oxford he assumed the professor's life had been the placid one of a scholar.

Until he learned who Dr. Benjamin Hartman was.

Quinn's mind was a jumble of memories as he sat down across from a man somewhere north of ninety years old. The clear gray eyes looked him over with polite curiosity.

"Mr. Quinn, if I recall, you attended Oxford as a Rhodes Scholar. Did you receive your Masters?" The voice had grown raspy but kept its cultivated manner.

"I did, sir."

"May I ask, in what field?"

"Politics and International Relations."

"An intriguing choice." Dr. Hartman's face lit up with interest. "I am interested in your thoughts on the world in these times, when parts of the globe are..." He paused for a drink of whiskey.

"On freaking fire?" Quinn sipped his beer.

"That does sum it up," replied Hartman drily. His lips pursed in a wry smile, and the eyes sparkled at the banter. "Where shall we begin?"

The conversation flowed as if they resumed a discussion begun in the Oxford coffeehouse. At times their talk was so lively they finished each other's thoughts. The pace would ebb when Hartman, using his beloved Socratic method of dialogue, posed a question designed to stimulate critical thinking, and then pick up again as soon as Quinn responded.

The girl watched them with amusement, rolling random balls so they banked off a gold diamond and into a pocket. After a few minutes, she shrugged, wandered back to their table, and waited expectantly.

Professor Hartman cleared his throat as they stood. "Rebekah Adler, please meet a former student, Mr. Michael Quinn."

Quinn grasped her extended hand. It felt delicate and feminine. He held it lightly, as he would hold a small bird. Beneath her visor, honey-brown eyes looked him over.

"Remember, you're going to show me how to play pool." She was still holding the cue.

"I promise, in a few minutes. Please join us." Quinn pulled a chair over from another table and they sat down.

Dr. Hartman swirled the ice in his glass of whiskey. "Rebekah is the granddaughter of an old friend. Her passion lies not with world events, but with mathematics. She is on her way to Stanford to start her Ph.D. program. As my travels also take me there, I have agreed to be her chaperone."

Rebekah patted the old man's arm. "Professor, you're too modest. Your trip to Stanford is also to receive a prestigious humanities award. Look, it's even made the news." She pointed to the television monitor on the wall behind the bar.

The local news showed video clips of the professor's career. Recent footage showed him speaking at the United Nations and before Congress, while a scroll at the bottom of the screen read:

"Dr. Benjamin Hartman, eminent historian, renowned Holocaust scholar, to be given Stanford University's famed Lifetime Achievement award…After receiving Nobel Prize ten years ago, Stanford award to cap professor's distinguished career…praised for his lifelong defense of freedom…ceremony to be attended by leaders from around the globe."

The screen changed to a series of old black and white photographs. Some were engaging, and some were bleak, from one of the darker periods in history. The scroll read: *"Captured by Nazis while still a teenager…sent to death camp…Hartman led inmates in daring midnight escape from the Nazi concentration camp."* The montage ended with Hartman speaking a month earlier in Switzerland, with the scroll: *"Holocaust scholar warns that history repeats."*

The news anchor then showed a brief photo of the Lifetime Achievement award plaque. Quinn caught the words "enduring contribution to humanity" and then the screen cut to the weather girl, pointing to a live video feed from a shorted-out power station.

The picture flickered, and the restaurant lights dimmed as rain pummeled the shingled roof.

Rebekah sighed. "We were going to drive straight through but got waylaid by this stupid storm. Now we're stuck here for the night."

"There are far worse places." The professor shifted in his chair as the lights brightened. "Mr. Quinn, thinking of Rebekah reminds me that you were also a promising student. What direction has your career taken since Oxford?"

Quinn thought for a moment. "In a sense, it changed because of your class."

"How so?"

"Do you recall that late-night coffeehouse session when you recounted your escape from the Nazis?"

"I do."

"That evening became a turning point for me."

Rebekah leaned forward. "Oh! Professor, I've always wanted to hear the story of your escape from that Nazi death camp. My grandfather? I couldn't get two words from him about it. He would always change the conversation when it came up."

Hartman shook his head. "It is not a subject for conversation with a young lady."

"Professor, I'm twenty-one, not fourteen."

"It is not pretty."

"You've always urged me to take an interest in history, pretty or not. And tonight, with us cooped up in here seeking shelter from that horrible storm outside, you've got a captive audience." She leaned forward, imploring. "Please, Dr. Hartman, this evening was meant to be."

"Mr. Quinn, you have no objection to hearing it again?"

"To the contrary, sir, its lessons are timeless." Quinn glanced at Rebekah. 'And I agree with the young lady that this occasion, where our three paths have crossed in this out-of-the-way place, is fortuitous."

"Very well, then." Dr. Hartman's eyes closed for a few seconds, and when they opened they looked out the windows, at something far away.

Outside the storm raged on, unforgiving. Rain hammered the ground and clattered against the window glass. Yellow-white lightning arced somewhere over the mountains, followed by distant thunder.

The old man spoke in a matter-of-fact tone. "I was not yet sixteen when the invading Nazis rounded up everyone in my village and shipped us off to a concentration camp. You already know what most people know, from popular culture, of the cruelty of daily life in these Nazi camps, so I will avoid unnecessary detail."

His eyes narrowed. "What brought my life there to a flash-point, however, was one particular guard. He was a member of the *Schutzstaffel,* the SS, and was sadistic beyond the norms of even his profession. He had a habit of coming into the prisoners' barracks at night and brutalizing the inmates. In the barracks, he would perform mock inspections, boasting that he had the power to torture and kill any of us at will if he found an infraction.

"There was this ring on his finger, a ring with a death's head insignia on it. He bragged that the ring meant that he was in the elite *Einsatzgruppen,* which massacred entire villages of civilians in Poland. Some they tortured and shot, some they burned alive in their homes. So proud of that, he was! He would grin and tell us that executions had become a pleasure sport for him."

Quinn's grip tightened on his beer bottle. Once, in class, the professor had rolled up his shirt sleeve and showed the numbered tattoo on his forearm to shocked students.

The professor continued. "Then, to prove his point, this SS guard would find an infraction, choose an inmate at random, and pistol-whip him.

"The other inmates knew to keep quiet. Ah, but I was

young and headstrong. One night, I lost it. I was shaking mad, and I yelled and cursed at this man."

Dr. Hartman looked down at the amber liquid in his glass. "He walked up to me, shoved me, and said I was finished. He brought his face up close and said that to make an example of me, the punishment would not be pistol-whipping. It would be execution by hanging. He spat at my feet and left."

"What a monster..." Rebekah spoke the words softly, almost to herself.

Hartman sighed. "I lay in bed that night, scared and angry at my foolishness. Then I realized I was going to die in that camp if I didn't escape. It was time for action.

"The next evening that SS guard barged into the barracks, later than usual. We were all in bed. He stank of alcohol, and when he yelled and cursed his words slurred. My bunk was towards the back, and he picked a prisoner near the front for that night's taunting and beating."

Dr. Hartman sipped his whiskey, re-living the night.

"I had my clothes on under my sheet. On the floor beneath my bunk was a twenty-pound sledgehammer I had pilfered from work. When he bent over to pistol-whip the prisoner, I ran up behind the guard and, with all of my strength, swung the sledgehammer into the back of his head.

"The force of the blow crushed the man's skull, and he crumpled to the ground, dead. I had been frightened, but at that moment my mind cleared. Now there was no turning back. Moving quickly, I relieved the guard of his P08 Luger and spare magazine, then I shoved his body under a bed."

Rebekah caught her breath as a shudder rippled through

her upper body. Quinn touched her arm, and she nodded that she was okay. The professor glanced at her, then he continued.

"I had a weapon, but I needed a distraction to occupy the other guards on night duty before we could make our escape. I told the other prisoners to be ready and wait for my shout.

"I slipped out of the barracks, keeping low to the ground, and ran to the motor pool in a back corner of the camp. There was a massive gasoline tank there, and several fifty-gallon drums. I opened a drum of gasoline and poured its contents under the tank, rolling it backward to make a trail of fuel. I lit the fuel with a cigarette lighter, and with a *whoosh*, the tank was surrounded by leaping flames. Then I took the guard's Luger and fired it at the tank."

Hartman glanced down at his hand, curled around his glass. The hand that had once held the Luger was now gnarled and speckled with age spots. "It took a few rounds, but the resulting explosion was so massive, it set adjacent buildings and vehicles on fire. It even knocked out part of the camp's electricity. As I sprinted back past the barracks, I yelled, and my fellow prisoners poured out."

Dr. Hartman gazed out the window at the storm, whose unrelenting downpour surrounded the Paradise. The rain pounding the roof and the winds howling all around seemed purposeful, as if trying to break in.

"It was winter and bitterly cold. We ran for our lives toward a section of the boundary fence in darkness from the electrical outage. In the distance, we could hear the guards yelling to each other.

"When we reached the barbed-wire fence, guards shouted orders to send out a search party. They had found our empty barracks. I had a pair of wire-cutters and cut through the barbed wire. Since it was my escape plan, I felt responsible. I decided to stay until all of the prisoners made it through.

"About half of them were through the fence when the searchlights from the watchtowers clicked on. Alarms sounded and sprays of machine gun fire from the towers blasted the ground closer and closer. But by the time the searchlights found the opening in the fence, we had all made it into the surrounding forest."

Dr. Hartman finished the last of his whiskey. "The Nazis launched a massive manhunt, but we kept going. We ran for miles and eluded them. Fortunately, we found friendly villages and, in brief, dispersed until after the war." He set his empty glass on the table with a soft *chink*.

Rebekah had been sitting hunched forward with her arms on her knees, listening intently. She exhaled and leaned back in her chair. "Such horrible times. It's hard to believe they really happened."

"They did," replied Hartman.

"We are fortunate, then, to live in this modern age. Such barbarities are obsolete and will never happen again." Rebekah picked up the pool cue. "That is why my interests do not lie with the past. They lie with the future."

Quinn looked at her. "Ignorance of the past can be dangerous. It can lead to indifference about the future."

Hartman looked at them both. "And indifference can lead to oblivion."

The girl opened her mouth to reply but gasped as lightning flashed outside the Paradise. Huge jagged bolts streaked from sky to earth, followed by a thunderclap so loud the ground trembled beneath them. Rain crashed against the windows like buckshot. The table was silent as they listened to the thunder recede and the storm return to its somber roar.

Rebekah regained her composure and tapped the cue in her hand. "Professor, thank you for the moving story. Now I believe I am owed a pool lesson."

Dr. Hartman smiled and ran a hand through his hair. "Please forgive the impertinence of the young lady. She is a free spirit." He looked at Quinn. "Before you go, young man, I am curious to hear about that turning point of yours."

Quinn put his beer bottle on the table. "Yes, of course. Well, when I started graduate school, I had plans for a business or academic career. But after that night at the coffeehouse, with all that was going on in the world, I realized that diplomacy and negotiating can only go so far.

"There are times when action is called for. When a warlord threatens your survival, the only thing that will get his attention is a warrior."

He looked at the professor. "At Oxford, there is a stone wall engraved with the names of the Rhodes Scholars who served in the two World Wars. I felt an obligation to serve my country as well and served six years as a Navy SEAL."

"Well done." Hartman nodded. "But I notice the past tense. Your service since then?"

Everyone at the table was silent for a moment. Hartman's eyes widened. "Of course! You are not at liberty to discuss your current activities. I understand."

The girl, a look of polite boredom crossing her face, pushed her chair back. "And I understand we have had enough history for one night." She stood and brandished her pool cue. "Now it is time for this new game." She put her hand on Quinn's shoulder and let her fingers drift down to his bicep.

Hartman sighed as he put his legal pad in a battered leather briefcase. "Very well, Rebekah. I am tired anyway, and ready for bed. I will leave your billiards instruction to the hands of this capable young man. But you will be in the cabin no later than eleven-thirty."

"Of course."

Dr. Hartman braced himself as he got up from the table and extended his hand. "Mr. Quinn, I hope our paths cross again." The gray eyes focused to take a mental photo, as if at his age, any encounter might be his last.

"Looking forward to it, sir." Quinn shook the firm grip and stood as the old man, slightly stooped, picked up a mahogany cane and made his way out of the lounge.

FIFTEEN MINUTES LATER, AN EXCITED REBEKAH HAD grasped the basics of pool. Quinn used the diamonds to execute a simple bank shot, and she clapped her hands and laughed, "It's basic geometry!" A few minutes later she gasped when, showing off, Quinn managed to pull off a Masse' shot and make the cue ball reverse direction.

Quinn had been put off by her brash attitude towards Dr. Hartman. Now, he decided, he'd been too censorious. Her playful love of learning showed that her outgoing nature was her *joie de vivre,* and he found her engaging.

"Michael, if I want the proper angle to bank the yellow

17

ball into the corner pocket, should I aim just to the right of that third diamond?"

"Yes. I can see your passion for math."

"Where else can you find a perfect world?" She watched as the yellow ball banked off the rail and rolled directly into the center of the corner pocket. "With mathematics, there's only one correct answer. You can attain absolute truth! In the liberal arts—history, philosophy, all of it—no one can agree on anything. What good is that?"

"What will you be working on at Stanford?"

"The Riemann Hypothesis. One of the great unresolved— ah, we can talk about that later." Her eyes met his. "I, Rebekah, hereby challenge you, Michael, to my first game of pool. My superior knowledge of geometry versus your skill sets." She removed her visor and looked at him with mock seriousness that dissolved into a grin. "An even match. But can you get me one of those cold beers first? It's getting warm in here. They must've turned the heat up." She turned around and began pulling her sweatshirt over her head.

Quinn walked to the bar and ordered drinks. The owner chatted him up, curious about the presence of such a celebrity. How well did he know the professor? Was that college girl famous as well? When he turned around with the two cold Negra Modelos, he took one step toward the pool table and halted.

The frumpy grad student had vanished. Quinn watched as Rebekah removed a hairbrush from her purse, leaned back and brushed thick, brown hair that hung to the waist of a very attractive woman.

Arching her back displayed a figure as slim and beautiful as that of a ballerina. Twin curves of milk-white breasts peeked from her low-cut tank top. Her flimsy top didn't quite reach to her low-cut jeans, revealing a tantalizing glimpse of a firm white waist.

She put her brush away, gave her hair a final shake, and smiled at him as she posed next to the pool table like a calendar girl.

"Michael, do I need to, what do you call it, break?"

"Yes, that's how you start. This is about the only time you'll want to put your body into it and hit the ball hard." Quinn walked over with the drinks and put them on a table.

"Can you show me?" She held out the pool cue and stood next to him, her gaze catching his. Up close and with the visor gone, her face was striking. Dark eyebrows arched high above her eyes, and below her delicate nose, her pouty lips were full. Her skin was flawless and almost the color of alabaster, befitting someone whose interests were cerebral and indoors.

Quinn put his arms around her taut waist and held her hands around the cue stick. The lemon fragrance of body wash or perfume teased his senses.

"Now!" He squeezed her hands and rammed the cue stick forward.

Rebekah squealed as the balls broke in a circle, and a striped ball rolled into the corner pocket. "Does that mean I'm stripes?"

"Yes, and you keep going. Now, if you hit the cue ball softly on the right side, you can knock those balls touching each other into the pocket. Hold the cue like this." Quinn stood behind her, wrapped his arms around her waist again and set her position. The lemon fragrance was intoxicating. As she leaned forward her cotton top rode farther up, exposing the pale small of her back and the even whiter curves of her posterior. Her soft skin brushed against him as she bent over and, after a deep breath, pushed the cue stick forward.

The cue ball spun smoothly on its axis and seemed to glide across the felt until it gently struck its target. One after the other, the two striped balls rolled languidly into the pocket.

"Yes!" Rebekah pumped her fist. She turned toward Quinn and, without warning, gave him a hug and a peck on the cheek.

Quinn mumbled, "Awesome." He gently put her arms back at her sides and stepped back, assessing the situation.

What was with the PDA? Could be just her natural exuberance. Some women were like that. Surely, she knew he was her *de facto* chaperone until she went to bed? That nothing was happening tonight?

Was it?

His body still tingled from her hug and kiss.

He glanced around the room. The elderly couples were at the register, paying their checks while making small talk with the owner. The men in coveralls lingered over their beers.

The rain on the roof reminded him that a couple of hours ago he'd been resigned to a cold and dangerous ride home. Now he was warm, dry, and savoring a Negra Modelo. A chance encounter had reunited him with a treasured mentor from his past. And he had made a new friend.

Paradise did not have to be complicated.

Rebekah tossed her hair back as she bent over and practiced her next shot. Her curves were prominent in the skinny jeans and cotton tank top.

Behind them, someone cleared his throat.

Quinn spun around, startled to see the four men in coveralls. He hadn't heard them get up. They stood a few feet away, facing him.

One stood in front, the other three grouped behind him. Their silence, rather than respectful, was hostile.

Quinn's instincts kicked in and he stepped forward, putting himself between Rebekah and the men, and assumed a balanced stance. Keep it civil. "What's up?"

"We're gonna shoot pool now. That's what's up." The apparent leader, a man with a shaved head and a scraggly chin beard, stared at him. Taller than the others at about six-foot-three with a wrestler's build, he flexed powerful arms.

Quinn held the pool cue in front of him as he looked the men over.

The four men wore gray coveralls with "Coast Cities Auto Repair" embroidered in black. None wore name-tags. The Alpha-male leader, with the chin-beard, had pale skin like an albino, but with a pallid, sickly-looking hue. Beads of sweat ringed his forehead and upper lip. His eyes were a yellowish-brown color that reminded Quinn of jaundice. He leered at the girl.

The yellowish eyes flicked back to Quinn, awaiting an answer.

"We're in the middle of a game." Quinn, mindful of the girl, kept his tone unchanged. "You can have the table when we're done."

Adrenaline coursed through Quinn's veins as he spoke. The situation in the lounge had, in seconds, taken a one-eighty. The mellow vibe evaporated, replaced by tension snaking

21

through the room like invisible fog. The body language of the four men—aggressive posturing and aggravated expressions—revealed everything he needed to know.

They were the only ones left in the room. The owner had gone through the kitchen's double doors, probably to close the motel office.

One of the other men in coveralls stepped forward. Shorter, with greasy black hair, he had the fit, wiry build of a tough street fighter. He pointed a finger at Quinn, displaying a forearm tattoo of the Grim Reaper. His voice was higher-pitched. "You don't own this joint, mister. You've had the table for a while. We're done eatin' and want to get in a few games before the old lady closes the place. You got a problem with that?"

Behind him slouched a lanky man with skull tattoos on his forearms and dirty brown hair sticking from beneath his baseball cap. Next to him stood the fourth man, pale and nervous-looking, with the furtive eyes of an addict. He used a finger to clean food off his gums, revealing the discolored, rotting teeth of a meth user.

Alpha, Street, Baseball-Cap, Meth. All had ex-con written all over them. Alpha had the height and reach, and looked like a brawler with a deadly punch. Street's likely speed and agility made him potentially even more dangerous. The other two were harder to gauge, but four against one was never good odds.

"You can have the table when we're done." Quinn kept his voice calm. "There's no need for trouble."

Alpha's expression darkened. This was a man not used to

being challenged. He licked the sweat off of his upper lip. The jaundiced eyes turned opaque.

Then the eyes flared and Alpha brought his arms up at his sides, gesturing to the men behind him.

Street, Meth, and Baseball Cap fanned out. Heads tilted back or to the side, and they shot Quinn various forms of stare-downs. Street edged further to the side, out-flanking Quinn on the left.

Alpha jabbed a finger at Quinn. "You're leaving now, man. But she gets to stay. She wants to learn how to play pool, right? She can play with us."

"Yeah, let the little lady here have some fun." Street's voice rose a notch. As he spoke he inched closer to her.

Baseball Cap moved toward her from the other side, outflanking Quinn on the right.

Alpha brought his hands up in a ready position, moving in like a boxer with a cornered opponent. The yellowish eyes taunted. "Hear that, man? You ain't in charge here, so get the hell back to your room an' leave us alone. We just invited the lady to party. An' I didn't hear her say no."

Street stepped closer to the girl, forcing Quinn to glance his way.

Alpha's right hand darted forward, reaching for Quinn's t-shirt. At the same time, Street reached for Rebekah. His other hand grabbed his crotch. "Hey sweet-cheeks, ya want some of thi—"

The word hung in mid-air as Quinn whipped the pool cue around and knocked Alpha's hand away, then pivoted and rammed the cue tip into Street's gut. Street doubled over, the wind knocked out of him.

Alpha yelped in pain and drew his hand back. Street, still doubled over, squealed as Quinn brought his elbow up into Street's nose. Street staggered back and fell to the floor, his hands covering his face.

A whooshing sound from behind signaled Baseball Cap lunging toward Quinn, his beer bottle swinging at Quinn's head.

Quinn's right leg shot out. The low sweep kick caught Baseball Cap behind the ankle just before his foot hit the ground. Baseball Cap's leg went up, and as he fell backward, Quinn turned and rammed the pool cue into his chest.

Baseball Cap hit the floor hard on his back. His hands went limp and the beer bottle rolled away. Quinn stood over him and pressed the tip of the pool cue into the dip of skin between the man's neck and collarbone. Baseball Cap coughed and made choking noises.

Alpha took a step forward and stopped, rubbing the red welts on his wrist. Meth was frozen in place. Street sat on the floor with a dazed expression, dabbing at the blood running down his lips and chin and staring at his bloody fingers.

Quinn caught Alpha's eye and pointed to the prone Baseball Cap. "This man's in serious pain right now." He pressed harder on the cue.

Baseball Cap gasped for breath. His eyes widened.

"The cue is pressing on his jugular notch," Quinn continued. "Probably no permanent damage has been done, yet."

Quinn ratcheted up the pressure on the cue stick. Baseball Cap's chest shuddered and he made retching noises.

The temptation to finish off Baseball Cap and quickly take

out the others flashed through Quinn's mind. But that would be messy and involve the authorities.

He caught Alpha's eye. "Here's the deal, badass. Clear your guys out of here, now. Or I crush your buddy's windpipe."

Alpha blinked. In a heartbeat, his demeanor changed. He seemed preoccupied, as if this incident was already in the past. "Okay, okay. No trouble, we're leaving. C'mon guys, we're outta here. Go!" he barked the order, still rubbing his wrist.

Quinn was taken aback by the quick surrender. He'd expected some trash-talk, a modicum of face-saving defiance. He stepped away and watched as Street wiped his bloody hands on his jeans and got to his feet. Baseball Cap rolled over on his stomach, got to his knees, and stood, one hand holding his throat.

Alpha motioned to the others and strode out the door, avoiding eye contact. Meth followed him, then the limping Baseball Cap.

Street stopped just before the doorway. He licked blood from his upper lip and glared at the girl. "We'll save you for later," he rasped.

He turned and closed the door behind him.

THE PARADISE MOTOR COURT WAS LAID OUT IN THE low-rise architecture from the days of inexpensive land. Behind the motel office and lounge, a covered walkway led past a swimming pool to a common area of grass and gravel, and then to the cabins, which were arranged in a long U-shape, facing each other.

Rain formed a silvery curtain as Quinn walked a pensive Rebekah along the covered walkway. The chilly night air was a relief from the sweat and tension of the lounge.

She moved closer. "Thank you for protecting me back there. Who were those men?"

"Just lowlifes. A type you will want to avoid."

"I hope so." Her voice faltered as their footsteps crunched the gravel.

"Forget about them. Tomorrow morning they'll be gone, and you'll have a leisurely drive up the coast."

"Sounds good. Now tell me, Michael, who are you?"

"A friend."

"No, I mean who are you really? I've never seen anything like what you did."

"I'm just a friend." He stopped at the end of the covered walkway. "Put your sweatshirt hood on and I'll jog with you over to your cabin. Here, hold my hand. Ready, go!"

She giggled as they splashed through the puddles, and seemed more like her previous self when they reached her cabin door.

"Well, thank you again, whoever you are, for teaching me pool and—everything." She pulled her hood off and faced him. She was panting from the jog and leaned toward him, her lips parted.

Quinn gave her a peck on the forehead. He liked her, but he wouldn't be seeing her again. He glanced out at the cabins. They were all identical, with a pitched roof, a window next to the front door, and a window on one side. "I'm in cabin number twelve, over there, just across the way from you. Let me know if you need anything. Lock your door. Good night."

"Good night, Michael."

―――――――

Thirty minutes later

RAINFALL USUALLY SERVED AS A SEDATIVE FOR QUINN, ITS rhythmic patter lulling him to sleep. Tonight was different. He tossed and turned and punched his pillow, trying to find the right position. He lay on his side and looked around the small room, at the couch across from his bed and the hotplate and coffeemaker on a table next to the tiny bathroom. Finally, he lay on his back and stared at the acoustic ceiling, listening to the rain drum on the shingles.

Maybe it was the severity of this storm which kept him awake. Or maybe it was the odd sense of unfinished business from the Paradise Lounge.

We'll save you for later.

What the hell was that about?

And there was more. Alpha had backed off too quickly in the lounge. This was something beyond the behavior of the typical sociopath. It was an I-know-something-you-don't arrogance, and it was disturbing.

He picked up his cell phone and surfed the net. With the remote area and the storm, the green signal-strength bars maxed at a shaky three out of five. Websites were slow to appear and quick to drop out. He typed in a search for Coast Cities Auto Repair.

His jaw tightened when a group photo of the four men opened on the business website. Their smiles looked as phony

27

as a day is long. But the website looked legitimate, down to the testimonials. Their company van had been one of the few vehicles in the parking lot. Their cabin was down at the far end of the U-shape, away from Rebekah's.

We'll save you for later. An empty threat from a drunk. His fingers punched in a phone number.

"Michael, you realize it's after two a.m. here on the east coast?"

"If you have a date, Will, tell her this won't take long. Need a quick search."

"I was sleeping, dammit. And where the hell are you? My GPS is tracking you in the middle of nowhere."

Quinn summarized his whereabouts, the evening, and his run-in with Coast Cities Auto Repair. "My gut says something is up with these guys."

"Do you have names? I've got their website up."

"No."

"We'll try facial rec software. The algorithms on our latest version are damn good, especially with full-frontal headshots like these. Call you in twenty."

Quinn killed time doing a search for Dr. Hartman. Links to articles from the New York Times and the Jerusalem Post appeared, and a biography on his author page listed his academic achievements, books and articles, and numerous awards.

A search for Rebekah Adler returned several namesakes. He narrowed the search by adding "mathematics" and there she was, all over social media. Her favorite game was chess, she had just read a great biography of someone named Hilbert, and her Facebook home page picture was a color photo of her on a white-sand beach on a sunny day, emerging from calm ocean shallows, her body dripping wet in a turquoise bikini. She was, from head to toe, a natural beauty.

He was enlarging the photo when his phone vibrated.

"Michael, your gut was right. All of these guys are felons who did hard time."

"Gang-bangers?"

"Not that I can see. Those tattoos are standard prison stuff, no gang affiliation. They all managed to offend society in separate ways. In fact, it looks like they led separate lives until they met up in vocational auto shop class in Folsom."

Will's tone sharpened. "The big guy, your Alpha leader, convicted on two counts of voluntary manslaughter. The one with the bad teeth, a long string of burglaries. The tall one with the baseball cap, armed robbery plus aggravated assault.

"And the one who made a pass at the girl? He's a piece of work. A serial rapist. Four arrests, two convictions, the other two times the women disappeared and never showed up to testify."

"How long have these guys been out of prison?"

"One to two years. And they've stayed clean since. Not so much as a parking ticket. They could have gone legit, you know."

"Will, stop channeling your inner social worker. Let's dig deeper. I think there's more. Start with the leader, the big guy."

"You got it. I'm wide-awake now, anyway. And if I find anything, it'll give me the pleasure of waking you up."

Quinn laid his phone on the nightstand and stared at the ceiling. He had done his due diligence. There was, in all probability, nothing there. In the morning, Rebekah would move on to Stanford, and he would enjoy a leisurely ride home with the sun on his back. He took deep breaths, letting his thoughts drift back to Rebekah's soft skin in that turquoise bikini.

Slumber clouds circled his consciousness. He was drifting off when someone knocked on his door.

A petite figure in a hooded poncho peeked in his window. The poncho's hood hid most of her face, but in the porchlight, he recognized her fair skin and full lips. He rolled out of bed and opened the door.

"Rebekah, what is it?" He scanned the surrounding darkness. She was alone. The porch light to her cabin was on, but the other porch lights were dark.

"I'm sorry to intrude, Michael, but I can't sleep. Dr. Hartman snores terribly, and we have two twin beds in one tiny room. I left him a note with your cabin number in case he wakes up. And frankly, I feel safer here with you. May I sleep here?" She glanced at his room. "I'll be fine on that couch. I won't be any trouble. And I promise to be gone first thing in the morning. Please?" Strands of her hair blew in the wind as raindrops pelted her cheek.

"I can give you some sleeping—" He stopped midsentence. The rap sheets of the men stuck in his mind, with a red light flashing at Street's multiple rape convictions.

The girl *was* safer here with him. Sending her back now bordered on negligence.

"Of course. I'll get you a blanket and pillow." He opened the door and let her in, then locked it behind her and turned out the porch light.

The musty smell of wet poncho and hair filled the small room.

"I really, really appreciate this." The girl flipped the hood back and smiled as she shook the rain out of her hair. Quinn unwrapped the plastic-covered spare blanket and pillow that lay at the foot of his bed. He was sprayed by raindrops as she lifted the poncho over her head.

"It feels so good to get out of this wet thing." Underneath the poncho she wore nothing but flip-flops, pink ladies' boxer shorts, and a white cotton tank top.

Inches away, her figure was revealed in exquisite detail, far beyond the glimpses allowed in the lounge. Her skin shone a soft pearl in the lamplight, with a delicious touch of pink. Pert breasts flared at him behind the thin fabric of the tank top.

"That's all the clothes you brought?"

"That's all I need to sleep. I'm better dressed than you are." She glanced at Quinn's navy boxers and took a longer look at his naked upper body. "You certainly keep fit." They almost touched as their bodies crowded the tiny room. Then her boxers brushed against him as she turned around.

"This will do just fine for a bed." She laid the blanket on the couch and the pillow on the armrest. After checking her cell phone, she turned it off and laid it on the floor next to her room key and poncho.

Quinn looked at the cheap lock on the door, then picked up one of the metal chairs from the dinette table and leaned it so the top jammed under the doorknob. From his duffel bag, he withdrew two screw-locks, placed them on the windowsills and screwed them tight. He opened a zippered compartment and removed his 9mm and its holster. He checked the magazine, cocked the gun and put the safety on, and laid it within reach under his bed. After a moment's thought, he removed the spare magazine and laid it next to the 9mm.

"Why do you carry a gun? Is it loaded?" She sat cross-legged on the couch and watched him.

"For protection, and yes, so don't touch." There was no point in telling her what he'd learned about the ex-cons.

She looked around the room. "What is that metal pitcher on top of the hot plate?"

He sat on his bed. "It's an old-fashioned kind of coffee maker called a percolator. Makes pretty good coffee, if you like it strong."

"We must try it in the morning. Everything in this motel is so old-fashioned and funny. And what's that metal thing attached to the head of your bed? The one that says 'Magic Fingers'?"

"Another relic from the past. You put two quarters in the slots and it vibrates the bed for a few minutes. Sort of massages you."

She glanced at the pile of pocket change on his end table. Her eyes caught his, and she leaned forward, her tank top exposing the deepening "v" between her breasts. "Then we should certainly try that. You look a bit tense. It'll help us sleep."

She picked up two quarters from the pile of change and dropped them in the slots of the metal box, then sat next to Quinn on the bed.

A metallic hum filled the air as the bed gently vibrated.

"Oh! Doesn't that feel good?" She snuggled up against him.

"That does it." Quinn got up from the vibrating bed.

Why hadn't he known better than to buy her story and let

her in? He grunted as he removed his gun and spare clip from under the bed and tucked them under the couch.

This was no time for her adolescent silliness. He had to get her safely through the night. He turned off the lamp next to the bed, and the small room plunged into darkness. The vinyl couch cushions were clammy as he lay down and pulled the thin blanket over him. "I'll take the couch. We won't need any help going to sleep. And speaking of sleep, it's time. Good night, Rebekah."

"Well, goodnight, then," Rebekah giggled as she pulled up the bed covers.

He lay on the couch, and she lay on the bed, both facing the front window. The bed stopped vibrating, and they listened in silence as rain beat on the roof and splashed against the glass.

With his gun by his side and the girl locked in his cabin, Quinn's small section of the universe now felt safe. Outside, lightning flashed in the distance and the thunder rumbled quietly. The storm was making its way west.

The falling rain finally soothed his soul. He turned on his side and fell asleep.

One hour later

THE MUFFLED SHOUT MIGHT HAVE BEEN PART OF A dream.

Quinn awakened with a start. He lay still on the couch, sorting out the sounds around him.

Across the room, Rebekah was asleep on the bed, making soft breathing noises.

Maybe the noise was just the falling rain. Its patter was like chanting voices huddled outside, warning about something. He focused his hearing and isolated the plop-plop of raindrops on puddles and the gurgle of an overflowing gutter.

His ears perked at the sharp sound of breaking glass.

He lifted his head and looked out the front window. His eyes adjusted and he made out the tall shapes of the palm trees and the outlines of the cabins. The scene was darker than before.

Rebekah's cabin porch light was off. Perhaps the old man had awoken and turned it off.

From somewhere outside came another muffled shout, and then a grunting noise, lower-pitched, from a different man's voice.

Quinn rolled off the couch and crouched below the window. He pressed his face near the glass, straining to see through the muted shades of black and gray.

The skin on the back of his neck crawled when he saw that the door to Rebekah's cabin was ajar. It moved in the wind, letting the rain inside. Her cabin was dark.

His stomach churned as he realized the Paradise's complete lack of security. Behind the cabins was a large asphalt parking lot, with a parking space behind each cabin. And beyond that? Vacant land, unfenced, leaving the complex wide open to intruders.

A shape to the right of her cabin caught his eye. Outlined by the slanting rain, it was black and square, about as wide as it was tall. The strange-looking form moved to the right, floating like some sort of phantasm toward the farthest cabin.

Quinn unscrewed the lock and slid the window sideways, opening it. Now footsteps crunched in the gravel outside. Whatever it was, it was not floating, and it had legs. A close examination revealed round contours at its top. The curves of human heads.

Below the heads were the curves of shoulders and torsos. The thing was two humans moving together. No, three. The two humans on the ends were carrying the smaller one in the middle. They moved as a group and headed directly toward the farthest cabin, the one at the bottom of the "U".

Quinn's eyes further adjusted, and he made out the dim outlines of arms and legs. The bodies of the humans on the ends looked familiar. The man in the middle was struggling and indistinct. He shouted something whose words were garbled by the roar of the storm.

But the voice was as unmistakable as it had been in the Paradise Lounge. The man in the middle was Dr. Hartman. He was pinned between Alpha and Street.

They were only steps from the cabin. Beyond it was parked a commercial van. The van that had "Coast Cities Auto Repair" on the sides.

They came for the girl.

Quinn's mind raced as he pulled on his jeans, tee-shirt and boots. The men broke into Rebekah's cabin and found she wasn't there. Did they find Rebekah's note? Then they knew where she was and would come for her. Were they taking Hartman hostage to get the girl?

35

He grabbed his phone. *Call 911. Get Hartman to safety. Hold the four men until the police come.*

The blank screen stared up at him. Was the damn thing dead? He pressed the power button, and the tiny light glowed in the center, signaling a boot-up.

Who'd turned his phone off? He always left it on. This wasted precious seconds. He watched the maddeningly slow process as the phone came to life.

A red light on his phone blinked, signaling urgent texts. Another light showed three missed calls. He frowned as he waited for the texts to download.

Where are you?

His phone vibrated as the next text came in.

URGENT CALL ASAP

The screen darkened as the signal dropped out. Quinn looked up, waiting for his phone to connect again. Muffled voices and a heavy thump cut through the sounds of the storm. He looked out the window to see the front door of Alpha's cabin open and the three men disappear into it.

His phone vibrated as more of Will's texts downloaded.

Hacked home computer of Alpha leader.

The girl stirred. She yawned and turned over. "What's going on?"

"Don't know yet. Did you turn off my phone?"

"Yes. It kept vibrating and waking me up. I didn't want it to wake you. I felt guilty about bothering you, so I turned it off so you could sleep. I always turn mine off when I go to bed, don't you?" She sat up in bed. "Is something wrong?"

Quinn broke into a cold sweat as his phone continued to buzz with each of Will's text updates.

All four men are jihadists. Homegrown. Radicalized while in prison.

Hiding in freaking plain sight. Terror attack planned.

The door to Alpha's cabin opened, and the silhouette of a man wearing a baseball cap emerged. Quinn's heart hammered as his phone vibrated with more texts.

Terror attack planned for San Francisco landmark.

Large quantities of explosives stored in Oakland warehouse.

Locations unknown.

Baseball-Cap stood guard in front of Alpha's cabin. He turned slightly, revealing the silhouette of a rifle with a circular, high-capacity drum magazine.

Quinn's phone vibrated as additional texts downloaded.

Indications attack may be imminent.

FBI and police alerted but with weather and distance ETA to your location two hours plus.

Apprehend and detain all four hostiles ASAP CONFIRM CONFIRM

The "dammit" was left off. He was texting a reply when his phone vibrated with a phone call.

"Will, I'm on—"

Will cut him off. "Michael, can you see their cabin? Do you see a light?"

"A bright light just appeared in the side window. How did you—"

"We're scanning the whole damn motel. That's the video light from one of their phones. Hold on, I'm patching you in." There was a pause, and Quinn heard Will talking on another line, then he came back. "Check your screen."

A bright, color video feed filled Quinn's cell phone screen.

37

Dr. Hartman stood in the corner of a room wearing a white tee-shirt, his hair in disarray and his face flushed red. His gray eyes stared at the camera with defiance. The sharp steel blade of a machete pressed against his throat.

Alpha stood behind Hartman, his beefy arm wrapped around the professor's neck and his hand firmly gripping the machete. Alpha was speaking to the camera. Blood dripped from his right cheek, and there were several small cuts as if a piece of broken glass had been scraped down it. Dr. Hartman had fought back.

"Michael, we picked up their conversation. They're on their way to Oakland to pick up the explosives for their San Francisco attack. Damn these bastards, they're talking about taking out hundreds of civilians. They've been planning this attack since they were in prison. Folsom is a hotbed of this jailhouse jihadist garbage." Will took a breath and lowered his voice. "Their target right now, though, is Dr. Hartman."

"Why are they after Hartman?"

"They're going to execute him as an infidel. It's a freaking crime of opportunity, Michael. They found out who Hartman was, and that he's world-famous, from that television newscast in the lounge. By killing him, they can send a shock wave around the globe and make themselves known before their big event."

"And the girl?" Quinn glanced across the room. Rebekah sat upright on the edge of the bed, listening to every word. Her eyes were wide with fear and her knees shook.

"She's just a bonus to them. She's entertainment. When they saw Hartman leave her alone with you, they figured all they had to do was get rid of you and they would have the girl all to themselves after they got rid of Hartman.

"Right now, the leader is giving a speech to the camera. When he's done, they're going to behead Hartman, then upload the damn video for the whole world to see."

Will paused, and Quinn sensed controlled fury in his voice when he spoke again. "Neutralize them, Michael. Any means necessary,"

"Copy, out." Quinn tucked the phone into his back pocket.

"What are—" Rebekah went silent as he raised his hand.

He tucked his 9mm into his waist holster and put the spare magazine in his pocket. He reached into the back of the duffel bag to a zippered compartment, withdrew his suppressor, and screwed it into the barrel of his 9mm. Next, he removed an innocent-looking pouch which contained an M67 hand grenade and clipped the small pouch to his belt.

"Stay here and keep the door locked. I'll be back." He looked around the room at the rectangular window above the couch. It faced away from the front of the cabin and appeared big enough to crawl through. He climbed onto the couch, unscrewed the lock, and slid the window sideways, opening it. Next, he popped out the screen and laid it on the couch. One leg on top of the couch and the other on the windowsill, he climbed through, perched on the sill, and jumped.

He landed in muddy grass. Wind whistled around him and chilly rain pelted his hair and skin. Ignoring his soaked clothing, he crouched and peered around the corner rain-gutter. Baseball-Cap stood guard in front of the men's cabin, his rifle at the ready.

Quinn drew his 9mm. He had seconds, maybe a minute, before they executed Hartman. He scooped up a handful of wet rocks and put them in his pocket. His plan, though rough, was complete by the time he aimed his 9mm.

Say goodbye to freaking Baseball-Cap.

The 9mm spat three times. The silhouette of Baseball-Cap twitched like a marionette, then crumpled to the wet ground.

Quinn was already running through the grass toward the men's cabin. He'd gambled that the noise inside their cabin, plus the noise from the storm, would drown out his gunfire and movement. No one came out the front door to see what had happened to Baseball-Cap.

Now to stop the execution.

The cell phone video had shown Hartman in a rear corner of the room, with Alpha holding the machete to his throat. Quinn ran past Baseball Cap's body to the side of the cabin, stopped and aimed through the side window at the bright light in the opposite corner of the room. He fired four shots, hoping to hit the head and torso of the cameraman.

The window shattered and the light bobbed crazily, then went dark. Shouts rang out.

The tip of a rifle barrel poked out of the window and knocked out the remaining window glass. Quinn holstered his gun and sprinted the short distance to the back of the cabin. A burst of automatic fire thumped the ground behind him, another nipped at his heels, and then he made a running leap to the top of the grey metal power meter adjacent to the rear corner of the cabin.

He landed with both feet on top of the rain-slicked meter and leaped straight up toward the cabin roof. The three-foot-tall meter gave him just enough of a boost to grab the edges of the shake shingles. A piece of a wet wood shingle broke off in one hand, but the rest held, and he hauled himself up and onto the steeply pitched roof.

He crouched on all fours, trying to distribute his weight evenly and be as light as possible. The winds tore at him and rain slammed into his face, but his fingers found a firm grip on the rough edges of the wet shingles. He crept his way along the roof peak, up to the front of the cabin. Shouts and curses poured through the broken window below him. The men inside were arguing about what to do next.

Quinn straddled the roof peak, drew his 9mm, and peered over the front edge. With the camera light out, everything had plunged back into darkness. Baseball-Cap's corpse lay in a heap in front of the door, raindrops glancing off of his body and into muddy puddles.

Quinn grabbed the rocks from his pocket and tossed them against the outside wall above the side window. A rifle barrel poked out and sprayed automatic fire. At the same time, the front door opened and another rifle barrel appeared, firing side-to-side.

The head and shoulders of Meth cautiously leaned out of the doorway, and his rifle spat longer bursts.

Quinn fired two shots directly onto the top of Meth's head. Dark mist sprayed in all directions and Meth fell forward, dropping his rifle as he collapsed over Baseball-Cap's body. He landed face down on the wet ground and lay still.

Two down, two to go. Quinn removed his empty clip and inserted his only spare. He would have to conserve ammo.

The world exploded around him.

Quinn sprang up into the air as blasts of rifle fire echoed on all sides. Pieces of wood and drywall ricocheted off him and flew in all directions as the gunmen inside raked the entire roof, side to side, and then front and back, with dozens of rounds. Twisting his body to avoid the fusillade, he came down at an awkward angle on the slippery edge of the roof and half-jumped, half-fell to the ground on the side of the cabin.

He landed hard in the wet grass and rolled. Pain shot up his left ankle, and his thigh burned. But he lay in darkness at an angle where he would be difficult to spot in the rain. He spat mud out of his mouth and aimed his 9mm with both hands at the front entrance. His bare arms shivered in the cold. He took a deep breath and focused on keeping them still.

The front door opened, and rifle fire blasted the entire area in front of the house. Quinn watched as three men exited the front door. Alpha was in front, the machete in a sheath strapped to his thigh, and Street was in back. They held Hartman, who seemed to have gone limp, tightly between them, and Alpha and Street each cradled a rifle in their outside arm. They fired staccato bursts as they stepped around the bodies of Meth and Baseball Cap and made for the parking lot behind the cabin.

Quinn couldn't get a clear shot. The receding target became a black blob in the darkness, and their cover fire kept him from moving closer. He rolled against the muddy outside of the cabin to minimize his visibility.

They headed toward the van, which was parked facing away from the cabin. He moved his 9mm back and forth as they made their way, looking for a shot, but it was hopeless.

All he could do was watch. If they got away, Hartman was a dead man.

Alpha shouted something at Street, who paused firing and reached in his coverall pocket, removed a small object, and pointed it at the van.

The van's taillights and headlights blinked on. The headlights shone on the empty parking lot. The red taillights, though dimmer than the headlights, produced enough pale, blood-red illumination to clearly reveal Quinn lying on the ground against the cabin. Raindrops splattered red in puddles around him.

"I got the bastard," shouted Street's black shape.

Street raised his rifle and aimed it at Quinn. As he raised the rifle he let go of Dr. Hartman.

The black shape of Dr. Hartman had been still. Now he sprang to life, twisting out of Alpha's grasp and giving Street a violent shove sideways.

Street stumbled three, four steps away from the other two. His silhouette was now separate from the others. Quinn fired three shots at the torso and head. Street yelled as the bullets hit. His rifle slipped out of his hands and splashed in a puddle. He slumped sideways, then fell to the ground and lay still.

Alpha screamed curses and blasted rifle fire in Quinn's direction. He grabbed Dr. Hartman in a headlock and dragged him toward the van, laying a steady stream of cover fire as he went.

Bullets splattered in the mud and thudded into the cabin wall behind Quinn. He rolled out of the pool of red light and into darkness, aiming his 9mm. The moving target was too indistinct and too far away.

The black form of Alpha holding Hartman moved in an arc away from him and toward the front of the van. Their path meant he would never have a clear shot at Alpha.

Quinn felt for the pouch and removed the grenade. He pulled himself into a crouch and estimated the distance to the van.

He grabbed the grenade's pull-ring with his index finger, twisted it, and ripped it out. One more look at the distance, and he used a side throw to lob the grenade. The grenade bounced once on the asphalt and rolled under the van.

The explosion lifted the van completely off the ground and sent orange and yellow flames high into the air. When Quinn lifted his head he saw massive smoke clouds billowing into the night and burning wreckage everywhere, the fires blazing fiercely despite the rain.

Alpha, still holding Dr. Hartman in a headlock, stopped and faced the inferno. Both men had their backs to Quinn. Alpha dropped the rifle he'd been carrying and unsheathed the machete strapped to his thigh.

Now.

Quinn sprang to his feet and sprinted forward. Alpha lifted his machete high in the air and shouted something. The machete was still pointing at the sky when Quinn got within range, dropped to one knee, and fired three shots at Alpha's head and upper body.

Alpha's shout became a bloodcurdling scream that echoed in the surrounding hills. His black silhouette dropped the machete. It took one heavy step forward, then toppled to the ground, still.

Dawn

"THE POLICE, CORONER, AND FBI HAVE ALL LEFT... ...No, just the girl and me now... She's asleep, gave her a sedative... Yes, I'll tell her."

Quinn leaned against the front porch of his cabin, a mug of black coffee in one hand, his cell phone in the other.

As he spoke, he watched the long night surrender to daybreak. Raindrops glistened on the wet grass around him. The cool morning air had the earthy scent that lingers after a storm has moved on.

"I'm fine. The back of the cabin absorbed most of the shrapnel. Flesh wound in the leg, twisted ankle. That's all. Paramedics patched me up... Of course not... Two hours or so... Thank you, sir... Copy, out."

He put his phone in his pocket and sipped the dark coffee, watching the golden sun peek over rolling green hills.

Footsteps sounded behind him.

The girl, wrapped in the thin blanket and holding a mug of coffee, walked barefoot onto the porch. Her face was pale. He gave her a reassuring smile.

"Good morning, Rebekah. I've got some good news. Dr. Hartman will be released from the hospital later today. Just cuts and bruises. Quite the stamina that man has. Says he will join you at Stanford in a day or two." Quinn watched her expression brighten. "And how is your first cup of percolator coffee?"

"With that news, it's the best coffee I've ever had."

She looked to her right. A broad circle of yellow tape surrounded a crime scene that, with its charred ground and piles of ashes and blasted remnants of the van, looked like something from an apocalypse.

Her voice grew somber. "I don't know how to say this, but after what happened, I keep thinking about evil people and the horrible things they do. I've read about them in news reports, of course, but they were always so far away. Evil was just an abstraction to me. Last night was the first time I've seen it first-hand. Now it's so real. What will stop it?"

"Whatever it takes."

"I thought you might say something like that." She turned away from the crime scene and looked at him. "And where are you headed?"

"South on PCH. Duty calls." He motioned to the duffel bag at his feet.

"We're going in opposite directions, then. I was hoping we could spend a bit more time together. Well, I guess this is goodbye." She extended her hand.

Quinn grasped the tender hand he'd first touched just the night before. A weight seemed to lift off his shoulders.

"Let's calendar in another time then, Rebekah. We should get better acquainted."

Her eyebrows raised in an are-you-serious look. "Well, you could visit me at Stanford, when you're up that way."

"Only if you let me take you to dinner at Te Amo."

"And that is?"

"My favorite Italian restaurant in the area. And you can tell me all about your passion over a bottle of Chianti." He picked up his duffel bag.

"My passion?"

"Your doctoral thesis, of course. I believe it is on the Riemann Hypothesis? You started to tell me about it last night. But, we got a bit distracted."

A breeze ruffled the girl's hair and lifted her blanket. She was still clad in her rumpled boxer shorts and cotton tank top. Goosebumps showed on the white curves of her slender ballerina's body. It was even more beautiful in the light of day.

She demurely put a hand between her legs, pulling the blanket back in place.

The corners of her lips turned up in a smile. "Michael, do you really want to hear about that?"

"Well, to start."

BALTIC DANCE

A MICHAEL QUINN SHORT STORY

KEVIN SCOTT OLSON

The principal instrument of the Anglo-American is freedom; of the Russian, servitude. Their starting point is different, and their courses are not the same, yet each of them seems marked by the will of Heaven to sway the destinies of half the globe.

— ALEXIS DE TOCQUEVILLE

BALTIC DANCE

Late night
Berlin, Germany

THE ICY WIND OF MIDNIGHT SWEPT THE DESERTED boulevard of *Eckestrasse,* tossing dust and scraps of trash in mad little spirals.

Michael Quinn turned up the collar of his leather jacket as he walked. The dingy sidewalks and concrete buildings of Berlin, which could be those of any big city at night, had earlier seemed cold and impassive. Now they were welcome. The solitude calmed his nerves.

Walking back to his hotel gave him time to decompress from the intensity of the last couple of hours. The chilly night air was a welcome break from the smoke and noise of the bar.

In the thick fog that hung low from the sky, the yellow street lamps looked like floating guideposts. *We will show you the way*, they signaled, *so you can be alone with your thoughts.*

His assignment in Germany was done. After some tense

vetting, things had gone as planned. Less than a half-hour earlier, in one of the tawdry bars a few blocks behind him, he'd successfully handed off the flash drive. It contained information so sensitive that no amount of encryption would suffice to have it sent through any kind of electronic communication. It could only be delivered in person, to one person.

Trusted soul to trusted soul, the Director had ordered.

Mission accomplished. Now all Quinn wanted was to go home. The drab Berlin cityscape held no attraction for him. He hunched his shoulders against the wind.

"Hallo."

The faint, feminine voice seemed to come out of nowhere.

Quinn whirled around.

At the far end of the block, red taillights glimmered as a black car turned onto a side street. The lights disappeared, and the boulevard was again empty.

The voice had probably echoed from an open car window. Quinn put his hands back in his pockets and walked on, thinking of his hotel room's warm bed.

Something moved in the mist, ahead on his right.

"Ich mochte partei?"

A dark-haired girl emerged from a recessed doorway. She stepped toward him, her breath exhaling like cigarette smoke into the air.

He stopped, curious.

She wore black fishnet stockings, a black leather coat, and black high-heeled boots. The coat was pulled tight against her shapely figure. She flashed an inviting smile.

But her eyes betrayed her. Dark and soulless, they were set

deep in bony sockets. The yellow street lamp illuminated the gaunt, prematurely aged face of an addict.

Her skin was sickly pale, and her shoulder-length hair, lipstick, and long nails were all colored a funereal black. Both wrists bore leather bracelets with metal spikes. The tattoo on her neck, of a rose-covered coffin, completed the picture.

A German gothic working girl. Not a sub-culture Quinn cared to hang with this evening.

"*Nein danke, fraulein.*" He shook his head and walked on.

Footfalls echoed behind him. The gothic girl was following. His eyes narrowed as she reappeared alongside him, matching his pace. They passed the last fading lights of the clubs and bars.

"*Amerikaner?*"

"Yes."

"Frahm whar?" She switched to broken English.

"California."

"Ah, *Kalifornien.* Vill you take me zare?"

"It's late." Quinn ignored her attempt to make eye contact and continued walking. Now they were alone in an area of dark buildings.

"*Nein,* it is never late in Berlin," the girl said in a faux-sultry voice. She linked her arm through his and pressed her body against him. The scent of her cheap perfume hung in the air.

Quinn extricated his arm and moved toward the street, his body tensing in case this was anything beyond what it appeared to be. A glance back showed no sign of anyone following them. The girl wanted one more score for the evening; that was all this was. He was about to tell her to go home when her hand took hold of his wrist.

She stopped, facing him. An alley with an overloaded dumpster was behind her.

Her free hand pulled at her belt, and her black leather coat opened, revealing alabaster-white breasts jutting out from a black leather bra. A silver navel ring glistened on her bare stomach. Her pierced tongue licked black lips as she tugged him closer.

Then her hand moved inside her coat pocket.

The ploy was beyond obvious. Quinn wrenched his wrist free and was braced and ready when a man dashed out from behind the dumpster. He focused on the knife in the man's hand. Then he startled at a sudden movement to his right.

"*Bastard!*" The girl spat the word and brandished a hypodermic needle and syringe taken from her coat pocket. She hissed something in German and waved the needle back and forth.

The man, powerfully built with a shaved head, charged Quinn while the girl moved nimbly to the side, as if choreographed. She jockeyed for position, looking for the moment to plunge the needle into his skin.

Quinn sidestepped and deflected the man's knife arm upward with his forearm, then jabbed his elbow hard into the man's face. The man grunted and tried to throw a counterpunch, but Quinn grabbed the wrist of the man's knife hand and, stepping forward, twisted it sharply toward the ground.

The man tripped and fell sideways, grabbing Quinn's jacket with his free hand. Quinn stumbled, and metal glinted to his right. The girl lunged at him, aiming the needle at his exposed neck.

His right leg shot out in a sidekick, and the steel cap of his shoe hit the girl's elbow. She shrieked, and her arm jerked up as she stumbled backward. The needle tumbled end-over-end through the air.

Quinn forced the man's arm down to the sidewalk. He stomped hard on the exposed wrist and heard the satisfying *crack* of breaking bone.

The man howled in pain and collapsed. His gloved hand opened and dropped the knife. Quinn heard footsteps and glimpsed the girl running away into the fog. He lifted the man by his shoulders and shoved him face-first against the dumpster.

The man grunted as his face collided with the rough-edged metal. He staggered, rubbing his face, and turned around, only to see Quinn's 9mm trained on him.

His face bleeding with cuts from the dumpster, the man spat and cursed something in German, then he darted down the alley and disappeared into the darkness.

The next evening
Hotel Luxe Central lounge, Berlin

"THAT WAS QUITE THE COCKTAIL THAT YOUNG LADY HAD prepared for you, Michael." Dieter, Quinn's contact in Berlin, placed his cell phone on the bar as he slid onto the barstool next to him.

"I'm more of a Scotch man." Quinn nodded at his Glenfiddich on the rocks.

Dieter ordered a Dunkles beer from the bartender and then scrolled the cell phone screen until he came to a photograph of the hypodermic needle lying on some sort of examining table under bright fluorescent lights.

"That may have been your last drink of any kind, my friend." His voice was soft-spoken. "What a mix of pharmaceuticals she had in there. They were designed to loosen you up so you would happily explain in detail everything you knew about anything."

"They thought I knew the contents of the flash drive. What was in that syringe, scopolamine?"

"Something much more potent. I'm not privy to details, but I believe a psychoactive drug similar to the Russian serum SP-117. It was laced with other chemicals whose nature is still undetermined. When they were done with you, of course, they would have killed you. We might have found your body in that dumpster."

"Fortunately, goth girls have never been my type. Anything on her or her boyfriend?"

"Nothing. No prints on the knife, and no security cameras there. This incident will just be a footnote to a successful mission. Perhaps you will learn not to talk to strange girls in such a rough part of town, yes?"

"Duly noted." Quinn sipped his whiskey. "And I assure you I have no plans to return there. Instead, I'm going for a run on a beach and a swim in the Pacific. I'm booked on the 7 a.m. flight home to California tomorrow morning."

"Not anymore you're not. A new assignment has just come in. Your field supervisor Will texted me an hour ago."

"Something here in sunny Berlin?" Quinn kept his demeanor calm, but his heart rate jumped, as it always did, with the challenge of a new case.

"You get to freeze your ass off a bit farther north." Dieter flicked the screen to a picture of a wide, smooth-flowing river flanked by rows of three and four-story buildings, all with the architecture of old Europe.

Yet not quite Europe. A majestic structure topped with golden domes and tall spires drew Quinn's eye. "Russia?"

"St. Petersburg, to be exact. With a stop in what might be new territory for you."

Dieter flicked his cell phone screen to a map of Europe. He scrolled up, past Italy, France, and Austria, until, just north of Germany and Poland, the map centered on the blue waters of the Baltic Sea. To the left of the sea lay Sweden and Norway, and to the right stretched the vast expanse of Russia.

Dieter's finger traced three small countries that bordered the sea on one side and Russia on the other. "Ever been to the Baltic countries—Estonia, Latvia, Lithuania?"

"No."

Dieter's finger stopped on the middle country. "Your first stop is in Riga, Latvia's capital. And your mission concerns something more interesting than a flash drive."

Dieter flicked the screen again, and an official-looking photograph of a young woman appeared on the screen. She had light brown hair, a fair complexion, and striking eyes— gray with a touch of blue.

Her facial features might have been pretty, but Quinn

couldn't tell because of her grim countenance. Her eyes weren't deadened like those of the German goth girl, but they were wary. Her mouth was drawn in a thin straight line.

"Meet Karina Lusis. Twenty-seven years old, a Latvian national, lived there all her life. Five-foot-eight, one hundred twenty-five pounds. Graduate *summa cum laude* of the University of Latvia. A linguist by profession. Fluent in seven languages, including English."

Dieter zoomed in on the image. "And for the past three years, she has also been a junior operative in the *Drosibas Policija,* Latvia's counterintelligence service."

"She should smile more."

"She is certainly not smiling now. She was kidnapped by the Russians last night."

"Was she running an op?"

"Yes. Working undercover in the eastern part of Latvia, near the Russian border."

"Why was she kidnapped?"

Dieter drank from his beer and sat back. "Big picture, Russia is looking to regain its lost empire. Russia's success in seizing land in Crimea and Ukraine has emboldened them to cast their eye on the Baltics, which they ruled under the old Soviet Union.

"The Baltic countries, of course, treasure their independence. They want to be part of a prosperous Europe, not a vassal of a resurgent Russian empire. NATO is aware of this and has moved additional troops into northern Europe.

"Russia doesn't want to trigger a full-scale war with the NATO countries. So they are playing small-ball against the Baltics: harassment, military intimidation, and kidnapping."

"How will this kidnapping bring Russia more territory?"

"They are using their Crimea playbook: use operatives to agitate and create a phony disturbance, in this case in Latvia near the Russian border. When the time is right, Russia will then declare that a 'preventive occupation' is necessary to restore order."

"And Russian soldiers move in?"

"Yes. And a slice of Latvia is seized and declared part of Russia."

"It worked for Hitler with the Sudetenland." Quinn looked at the map of the small Baltic country. It looked about the size of Maine. "But why did Latvia send a linguist on a risky op like that?"

Dieter ran his hand through his hair. "She was chosen for the op because she speaks fluent Latgalian, the dialect in that part of Latvia. Things had gone well. She had successfully infiltrated the cell of agitators and was preparing a report to expose them when the Russians apparently learned who she was, kidnapped her, and hauled her across the border into Russia."

"Is she being held for ransom?"

"On a grand scale. The Russians say she will be released unharmed if Latvia will allow the Russian troops in for their 'preventive occupation.' But Latvia won't agree to give up a piece of its country in exchange for a hostage."

Dieter looked at the dark brown liquid in his glass. "The Russians have already arrested Karina on bogus charges of espionage. If Latvia doesn't agree to Russian demands, torture and interrogation await her, followed by a show trial in Moscow and certain conviction."

"Latvia's a member of NATO now. What about exerting pressure with conventional diplomacy?"

"A kidnapping like this doesn't rise anywhere close to the level of what the NATO pact considers an attack."

Quinn swirled the ice in his drink. "Pretty shrewd. But doing nothing isn't an option for us. Inaction from the West will only be interpreted by the Russians as a sign of weakness."

"Precisely. And it could lead them to believe the time is right for a larger invasion. Reclaiming one of the Baltics for the Russian empire would stun the world."

Dieter fell silent and gave Quinn a knowing glance. There was no need to spell out what had to be done.

"So, we have a hostage rescue situation." Quinn finished his drink and let the weight of his new assignment sink in. "Where is she being held, and by whom?"

Dieter flicked to the next image. "In a small commercial warehouse on the outskirts of St. Petersburg."

His screen showed a run-down industrial area full of aging buildings and warehouses. He zoomed in on a one-story building with a single door in front and a roll-up steel garage door in the back.

Dieter opened another file. His face hardened as a photo of a man's face filled the screen. "Her kidnapper is a piece of work. Venedikt Kusnetsov. Former member of Spetzgruppa A of the FSB Special Purpose Forces."

"Former?" Quinn took in the man's hawk nose and the smallish brown eyes that stared back at the photographer. The man was in his mid-thirties, with a clean-shaven head and goatee that vaguely resembled Lenin.

"Yes. Drummed out of the special forces for sadistic cruelty."

"That shouldn't bother the Spetznatz. They're trained in bullying and beating."

"Yes, but Kusnetsov took it to another level. The FSB wants its operatives to kill as efficiently as possible and get out of there. Kusnetsov's modus operandi is torture. Not only on his enemies but anyone whom he felt crossed him. He prefers long, slow work with surgical instruments."

"Nice guy." Quinn scrutinized the photo and noted a faint half-inch scar above Kusnetsov's left eyebrow.

"Moscow keeps him at arms' length, sub-contracting him out for jobs such as this where his cruelty is an advantage." Dieter sipped his beer. "He's got three henchmen with him on this job. Two outside, guarding the building, and one with him, inside the building. You will need to neutralize all of them. The world will be a better place with them gone."

"What timeframe are we dealing with?" Quinn's jaw tightened. This wasn't going to be pretty.

Dieter tapped his fingers on the bar counter. "The Latvian government is stalling for time, and the girl is said to be unharmed, so far. However, as soon as Moscow decides Latvia is not serious—a couple of days, perhaps—they will give Kusnetsov the go-ahead to begin his torture."

"Dieter, you know that a hostage rescue like this usually requires a team of about twenty men. There'd be a perimeter team, an entry team, an intel specialist, a couple of snipers..."

"Michael, we can't run the risk. If things go wrong, it could literally mean war between nations. Russia is looking for any excuse to move troops in. And, we know you prefer to plan your own op and work alone. We will get you there and outfit you with whatever equipment you need. The rest of the op is in your hands."

"I'll make do. But just how do you propose to get me the 700 miles into St. Petersburg?"

A smile crossed Dieter's face. "You'll like this route." He glanced at an empty table in a dark corner. The bar area was getting crowded. "Let's move to that corner table and order another round of drinks."

Two hours later, Dieter sighed and sat back in his chair. His soft-spoken voice was tired and hoarse. "Okay, my friend, I think you are good to go. The op you are planning is, as expected, outlandish."

"And it just might work."

The next morning
Riga, Latvia

QUINN STEPPED OUT OF HIS TAXI ONTO THE cobblestone street of *Elizabetes iela* and was greeted by the delicious smells of fresh-baked pastries and dark-roast coffee.

His senses were tuned to soak up the first impressions of the new country. He'd kept his expectations low, preparing himself for a bleak land marred by poverty and the scars of its Soviet occupation.

To his pleasant surprise, he found himself strolling along the sunny, tree-lined streets of Old Town, an area as charming as any village in Switzerland or Austria. Friendly cafes and shops invited visitors to linger. The architecture was an attractive mix of old Europe, ranging from medieval to Art Noveau.

On the flight from Berlin, he had received the latest intel about the kidnapping of Karina, now well on the path to becoming an international incident. The Latvian government, displaying polite outrage, had sent several diplomatic notes to the Russian Ministry of Foreign Affairs.

Russia had not deigned to send a response. The Latvian government had then made "urgent" appeals to the European Union, the European Council, and the upcoming United Nations Human Rights Council meeting in Geneva.

Good luck with all that. Quinn walked toward the Old Town Bakery, the source of the wonderful aromas. *Perhaps type the next diplomatic note in capital letters.*

Bells hanging from a ribbon jangled as he entered the bakery.

Two young couples chatted at the back of the small establishment. An elderly, gray-haired woman sat at a front table. She was having her morning coffee and reading *The Baltic Times.* Her black and white coat was draped on the chair next to her.

Quinn greeted the pony-tailed waitress behind the glass display case and examined the savory display of Danishes, chocolate eclairs, and cupcakes. He settled on a slice of *Klingeris*—a type of coffee cake—and black coffee.

He sat at the counter and people-watched as he drank his coffee and consumed the delicious golden cake. It was a clear, blue-skied morning, and many locals rode bicycles or walked to their destination.

Quinn glanced up at a mirror hanging over a polished

espresso machine. Behind him, the old woman sipped her coffee and turned to page four of the *Times*.

Black and white coat on the chair, and page four of the newspaper. She was his contact, and the meeting was on. Some tools of his trade were impervious to technology.

He left the bakery and walked a block and half to a picturesque local park. Tall, shady trees bordered tidy lawns and flowerbeds of yellow and white daisies. Old men sat on benches while laughter echoed from a children's playground.

In the center of the park, a small wooden bridge curved over a winding stream. Quinn walked to the top of the bridge and waited, wondering about the dozens of padlocks affixed randomly to the bridge handrails. Many of the padlocks had brightly colored initials and hearts painted on them.

"Welcome to the Baltics, Mr. Quinn."

The old woman from the bakery appeared on his right, her tote bag and coat draped over one arm. Up close, her weathered, craggy face conveyed a dour expression.

She reached into her bag and removed a manila envelope. "Helena, at your service. Your papers are all here and in order. Passport, ship ID, even an itinerary of your cruise."

The woman spoke with crisp efficiency as Quinn examined the contents. "Per your instructions, your cover is as Mr. Justin Ridgeway, a prosperous American real estate investor, now a tourist on a luxury cruise to the Baltics and Russia."

"Looks like I've done pretty well for myself."

Helena looked like she'd been born with that stern look on her face. She nodded but did not acknowledge his attempt at humor. "Your suitcase is already on board. The other arrangements you requested have also been made."

She removed her cell phone from her bag and shielded it from the sun as she showed him a photo of a brown-haired thirtyish man with a mustache.

"This is Anton, your driver in St. Petersburg. He will meet you on a street near the dock, holding a sign with 'Ridgeway' hand-lettered on it. He will be driving a black Mercedes sedan.

"Anton has worked for us for some time and is completely trustworthy. For our purposes here, however, he is on a need-to-know basis. He has been instructed to take you to the safe house, to the point of extraction, to wherever you say, without asking questions. Beyond that, he knows nothing. We would appreciate it if you involve him as little as possible."

"Understood."

"Now, to our operative Karina." The old woman removed another manila envelope from her tote bag.

"She, of course, has no way to communicate with us, but I can give you a password that will let her know you are an ally sent to help her. When you first see her, you are to say 'It's a nice evening' in Latvian. Repeat after me: *Ta sirs skaists vakars.*"

Quinn did so, twice.

The woman nodded her head in satisfaction. "And she will reply, 'Unless it rains,' in Latvian, as follows: *Kad nau lietus.*"

Quinn repeated that as well.

"Good. Please use the password with your driver, as well. Be careful of conversation with anyone else. If you get into trouble with the authorities in Russia, we cannot help you."

Quinn thought of the map showing the tiny country and its belligerent neighbor. "I imagine there are times when you would just as soon land a division of Latvian troops in Russia and stop all this."

Helena gave him a sharp glance. She wore no makeup and, by her appearance, had long ago ceased caring whether the world noticed her age spots and homely features. In the sunlight, she could have been Mother Time, with a thousand lines etched deep in her face. Her shoulders sagged with the weight of many sorrows.

But when she spoke, her words showed a mind very much engaged.

"Of course we would. But that is exactly what the Russians desire. They would then claim to be the invaded country. And by the end of that day, my country, the Republic of Latvia, would no longer exist."

She gestured with pride at the well-kept trees and flowers of the little park.

"In this part of the world, Mr. Quinn, the dance with the Russians is done differently. We must take care with each dance step.

"Your United States was blessed to be born in freedom. My country has known independence for less than thirty years. Before that, we were conquered by the Russians, before that the Nazis, and prior to that the Russians again.

"Beyond our borders lies constant danger. We cherish our liberty dearly, and—" her voice rose, "—we do not wish to be devoured by the Russian bear again."

She opened her mouth as if to continue, then she licked her lips and handed Quinn the envelope. "But this is not the subject for today. This envelope has Karina's papers; please examine them. Your ship, the *Sea Goddess,* begins boarding at 2pm. Is there anything else?"

Quinn felt the need to lighten her mood. "One thing. I'm curious about all these padlocks on this little wooden bridge. They have hearts, initials, little messages painted on them in bright colors. What are they all about?"

Helena's face creased into a smile. Her eyes moistened as she gazed at the array of locks adorning the bridge. "We are on Love Lock Bridge. It is an old tradition here in my country. Young lovers come here when they get engaged. They paint their name or initials on a lock, lock the padlock on the bridge, and throw the key in the water because they are to be married forever."

Quinn opened the envelope and looked at Karina's passport. It was in the name of Mrs. Jessica Ridgeway.

Helena extended a wrinkled hand. "Good-bye, Mr. Quinn. I imagine that this is your first mission in which your assignment is to rescue your wife."

The next evening
St. Petersburg, Russia

THE *SEA GODDESS* GLIDED THROUGH THE CALM WATERS OF the Neva River, moonlight shining on its wake of white froth.

The cruise ship's journey across the Baltic Sea, through the Gulf of Finland, and up the river had gone according to schedule. With the busy commercial traffic of the day gone, the elegant white ship had the river to itself.

Quinn stood on the top deck, happy to be away from the crowds that mingled below on the restaurant and lounge decks. It was a cool, clear night, and in the coal-black sky, countless stars shone in brilliant silver and white. These were the same distant points of light that had greeted seafarers hundreds of years ago, thousands of years ago. They would be there a thousand years from tonight.

He sipped his whiskey and watched the ship slowly pull into port.

Past a golden-spired cathedral, through an open draw-bridge lit in turquoise, the lights of St. Petersburg shimmered on the river like those of a beautiful underwater city.

What history that river had witnessed!

The magnificent Winter Palace came into view, its green and white baroque architecture bathed in amber light. Inside those Palace walls, Catherine the Great had dreamed of bringing her country into the modern era.

Inspired by the Enlightenment sweeping Europe, she founded universities and the Hermitage. She encouraged businesses to prosper with Adam Smith's ideas on capitalism, and she encouraged the arts by importing French plays and Italian opera. Her goal was nothing less than to develop her beloved Russia into a flourishing part of Western civilization.

But it was not to be. Russian history became a bloody and violent three steps forward, two steps back, culminating in the twentieth-century abyss of the Soviet Union.

Quinn watched the city lights grow closer. What if Catherine the Great's dream had come true? Then there might have been no World War I, no Bolshevik Revolution. No gulag, no Soviet empire.

Maybe no Kusnetsov to deal with tonight.

The ship's engines growled, and then Quinn felt a gentle bump. The ship was docking.

He glanced down at his crisply pressed slacks. Tonight was "formal night" on the ship, and he was appropriately dressed in black pants, a white tuxedo coat, a white shirt, and a black bow tie. His lips pursed at the contrast between his clothes and his actual plans for "formal night." He finished his drink and tossed the plastic cup in the trash as he went downstairs to join the disembarking passengers.

Tourists from several ships crowded the dock, off for an evening at the ballet, the opera, or the many restaurants along the glittering main boulevard of Nevsky Prospect. The crowd thinned as he walked a half block in the chilly night air to a darkened area, toward a man waiting in front of an idling Mercedes. The man held a hand-lettered sign that said, "Ridgeway."

"*Ta sirs skaists vakars,*" said Quinn.

"*Kad nau lietus,*" replied Anton the driver. He nodded and opened the back door of the Mercedes.

After perfunctory greetings, the ten-minute drive passed in silence. The safe house was a duplex at the end of a quiet cul-de-sac. Anton drove the car into the garage, closed the garage door, then motioned for Quinn to exit.

Up a cramped staircase, they walked into the living room of a modest two-bedroom apartment with the blinds drawn. Quinn's clothes and gear lay neatly on one of the beds. As he undressed and carefully laid out his evening clothes on the bed —he would be wearing them again—he glanced into the other bedroom.

On the other bed, also carefully arranged, lay a formal evening gown, shoes, and underclothing, all in Karina's size. Everything he had asked for was there, even the jewelry and a makeup kit.

In five minutes, he was dressed, head to toe, in black clothing. In addition to being non-reflective, the clothing also blocked infrared technology and was thus invisible to most night-vision cameras.

He took care, as he always did, with his gear. He strapped on his hip holster and drew his HK 9mm three times to make sure it didn't catch.

Next came his body-armor assault vest. Inside the vest pockets, he found the knife and spare magazines he'd requested. He put on the vest, packed the rest of his gear into a backpack, and adjusted the straps.

Last was the heavy artillery. He picked up the HK MP5 9mm rifle from the bed. It came, also as requested, with a suppressor and two attached 30-round magazines, clipped so he could quickly change magazines. The ammo was subsonic hollow-point, to minimize noise. He adjusted the rifle sling. Ready to go.

The drive to the target area also passed in silence. They entered an area of older industrial buildings and dark, empty streets. Anton dropped him off in an unlit alley two blocks from the target building, then the Mercedes purred off into the night.

Quinn looked around. The change in his surroundings was surreal. He was alone in a very different world from the bright lights and crowds of Nevsky Prospect.

This industrial area was even more run down than in the

photographs. The dilapidated buildings and warehouses that lined the alley looked to be from Soviet days. Some of the buildings were boarded up, and others looked abandoned.

The only sound was the din of the city, a faint roar of distant traffic and voices that sounded oddly like the ocean. As Quinn walked down the alley the sound was enough to cover his footsteps, as long as his boots avoided broken glass and metal scraps.

He saw no signs of life. Any business that could afford to move to greener pastures had long ago moved on. Neighborhoods, like humans, can grow sick and die. This was a dying neighborhood. The symptoms were its blight and decay.

Low clouds had moved in, shrouding the moon, and the resulting darkness was Quinn's friend. Most of the streetlights were out, either from lack of maintenance or from being shot out by vandals.

He stopped at the end of the alley, a block from his target. His breath formed white plumes in the chilly air. The temperature was dropping as the Russian night settled in. Gusts of wind swept down the alley, biting through his clothing.

What would he do if a police car turned the corner and lit him up with its headlights? He hadn't bothered with a cover story. Armed as he was, there was no plausible cover story.

Keeping close to the buildings, he made his way along the block until the target building was in sight across the street. As the photos had shown, it sat on a street corner. And it bore the only sign of life in the area: light shone from a small, barred window, blinds drawn, and from a skylight on the roof.

He found a recessed doorway that offered a full view of the building side that paralleled the street and a partial view of the rear of the building. He pressed into the back corner of the doorway and removed his night-vision binoculars from his backpack.

The one-story building looked just as drab bathed in green light. Brighter green light shone from the window and skylight. Somewhere at the front of the building was the guard stationed at the entrance. And somewhere else, also out of Quinn's sight, was the second guard, the roamer.

The building, he'd been assured, had no motion sensors or cameras. It was not barricaded, and there were no attack dogs, not even an alarm system. The kidnappers were confident in the obscurity of their location.

He looked at his watch and set the chronograph to count-down. Assuming the ship left St. Petersburg on schedule later tonight, he now had just under ninety minutes to complete the op.

He waited, shivering in the night air.

A green human shape carrying an AK-47 rounded the far rear corner of the building. The roamer.

The man walked at a slow pace along the back of the building, then turned and walked along the street side, away from Quinn. As he walked, the roamer's head turned from side to side, scanning the area. He stopped, spoke briefly into his cell phone, and then resumed his patrol.

Quinn used the binoculars to map out a clear path to jog across the street, then he tucked them in his backpack. At close range, the ambient light would be sufficient.

His fingers ran over his rifle and sling and moved it from his front to his side. He touched his holstered 9mm and tested his backpack straps. Finally, he gripped the textured handle of the stiletto-shaped six-inch knife hanging handle down, its blade sheathed, in a pocket in the upper front of his assault vest.

The roamer rounded the far rear corner again, walked along the back of the building, then turned the corner and started down the street side.

Quinn fast-walked across the narrow street, his footsteps silent. He slowed his pace as he turned and crept along the sidewalk directly behind the roamer. He unsheathed the knife.

The roamer's silhouette came into focus as Quinn closed in, now just a few steps behind. The roamer's head swiveled from left to right. The thick back of his neck offered itself.

In one motion, Quinn grabbed the roamer and pulled him close, clamped his hand over the roamer's mouth, and plunged the knife into the side of the roamer's neck and then forward. The roamer jerked and gurgled, and then blood spurted and his body went limp as the blade severed the carotids, bringing instant unconsciousness.

Quinn laid the roamer's lifeless body down on the concrete, wiped the blood off the knife, and hurried to the front of the building. He stopped and peered around the corner.

The entry guard was sitting in a folding chair, his back to Quinn. His AK-47 lay on the ground next to him. He held a lighter in one hand and a cigarette in the other. The man leaned back in his chair and brought the cigarette and lighter up toward his mouth.

The guard's arms jerked and eyes bulged as a hand covered his mouth and jerked his head back. The guard grunted as the knife blade plunged into the side of his neck. His legs kicked out and he made one feeble effort to rise, and then he slumped back in his chair, blood pooling on his chest. Both of his hands opened, and the cigarette and lighter dropped to the ground.

Quinn arranged the body with his head down and his hands on the lap so that from a distance it looked like the guard was resting in his chair or perhaps had nodded off.

He looked at his watch. Ten minutes had elapsed. How long until the roamer was due to check in again?

Get on with it. From his backpack, he withdrew the olive-colored plastic package that contained the door charge.

With a hostage situation, he didn't have the luxury of making a statement by blowing half the building in. The charge needed to be powerful enough to blast open the door but not so powerful as to hurl metal fragments that could harm the hostage.

Quinn had estimated the necessary explosive force of the charge based on Dieter's photographs of the front door. He unwrapped the package, removed the adhesive strip on the back, placed the charge on the door lock, and capped the charge.

Careful with each footstep, he padded around to the windowless side of the building, placed a second, smaller charge against the circuit breaker box, and capped it.

The light from the roof showed him the position of the skylight, his point of entry. He put down his backpack and removed the lightweight, telescoping ladder strapped to its frame. The ladder was small, but its carbon fiber composite would bear his weight, and its sixteen-foot reach would get him onto the roof.

He pressed the side button, and the ladder quietly extended to its full length. Then he leaned the ladder against the building, put on his backpack, and climbed.

The roof was flat and made of inexpensive composition material. He put one foot on it to test his weight, then rolled the rest of his body onto the roof's sandpaper-like surface, keeping his profile as low as possible.

On the rooftop, the distant golden lights of St. Petersburg glimmered through the clouds. Winds were stronger, gusting from all sides, trying to chill his bones. But their added noise would help cover any sounds he might make, as would the sound-deadening composition surface, with no concrete tiles to shift or wooden shakes to crack. He kept his head down and crawled to the rear edge of the skylight.

A thick eyebolt protruding from the roof caught his eye. He tugged at it, found it sturdy, then removed a coil of rope from his backpack and tied one end to it. He raised his head and looked through the skylight.

His heart thumped at the sight of the three figures in the center of the room. The harsh fluorescent ceiling lights illuminated them so clearly, it seemed Quinn could reach out and touch them.

All had their backs to him. The girl, in a white blouse and jeans, sat in a metal folding chair. Her hands were bound behind her back, her ankles were tethered to the chair, and her mouth was gagged. Her blouse was partially unbuttoned and pushed down past the bra strap that ran across her back. Her pale shoulders and upper back showed no cuts or bleeding.

The inside guard stood in front of the girl. His head and neck were outside Quinn's field of vision, but Quinn could see

75

the back and lower body of a stocky man dressed in a black coat and pants, holding an AK-47.

The guard turned to face the front door. Was he about to open it, to relieve the guard at the entrance?

To the right of the girl stood Kusnetsov.

Short and wiry, he wore a black tee-shirt and black pants. His shaved head glistened with perspiration. The butt of his 9mm protruded from his side holster. He turned to look at the girl, and Quinn confirmed his hawk-nosed profile and the small scar.

Next to the girl stood a small, stainless steel table holding a scalpel, a pair of needle-nose pliers, and a black taser with a pistol grip. The tools looked clean and unused, with no scraps of tissue or streaks of blood anywhere.

Quinn leaned forward and touched the skylight. It was, thankfully, glass, not plexiglass or the bullet-resistant acrylic used in modern structures. This glass would shatter easily. There was a danger that falling shards could harm the girl, but that had to be measured against the danger she was already in.

He punched in a code on his cell phone, watched the encrypted icon appear, and lay the phone on the roof.

He retrieved his fusion goggles from a zippered compartment in his backpack. Night-vision goggles with a thermal overlay, they amplified both the available light and thermal signatures. The orange outline of the thermal image would show anything that produced heat.

When Quinn slipped them on, they bathed the warehouse in the same green light as from his binoculars, but the three human shapes now burned in bright orange.

The wind picked up, sweeping across the rooftop and

rattling the vents. Quinn's chronograph showed he had seventy-one minutes left. His accelerating heart rate and increased blood flow told him it was crunch-time.

He leaned forward, took a knee, and aimed his rifle at the armed guard. While this exposed him, shooting down into the glass made for a more accurate hit. Then he could resume a prone position to take out Kusnetsov.

Quinn inhaled a deep breath and pressed the icon on his phone.

A double *bang* echoed around the building as the charges exploded, and the lights went out in the warehouse. The three orange-lit figures inside startled and looked at a small cloud of dust that spread inward from the front door.

Kusnetsov shouted something, and the guard stepped forward and aimed his AK-47 at the door.

Quinn fired a half-dozen rounds at the orange-lit guard. The skylight shattered as if hit by a giant hammer, and the piercing crash echoed through the night air as jagged shards fell straight down.

Kusnetsov dodged to the side and looked up. Quinn felt the man's cold eyes focus on him.

The guard stumbled as he was hit, but he didn't fall. He turned around and aimed his rifle up at the hole where the skylight used to be.

Quinn rolled to his side as the guard fired a stream of bullets across the skylight opening, shattering most of the remaining glass. As tiny glass shards fell to the roof, he cursed his realization that the guard was wearing a body-armor vest under his coat and was probably only wounded in the leg.

Staying just out of sight, Quinn turned on his side to look

through the opening. The warehouse was dark, but the fusion goggles showed the bright orange thermal outline of the three humans inside.

Kusnetsov brandished his 9mm and shouted something in Russian. The guard limped to the center of the room, aiming his rifle up at the skylight.

Quinn leaned in and fired a burst directly at the guard's head and chest. The rounds hit home, and the guard screamed and dropped his rifle, but Quinn had to duck away again as bullets from Kusnetsov's pistol hammered into the metal edge of the skylight and the roof. Quinn rolled farther away from the skylight, but more bullets tore through the roof around him.

Kusnetsov was following the sound of his movement.

Quinn froze in place and the gunfire ceased. He carefully rolled onto his stomach. With his weight on his elbows and toes, he lifted his body off the roof and slowly worm-crawled, making a wide arc around the skylight, toward the other side of the opening.

At any moment he expected bullets to rip through the roof and into his body, but the warehouse remained silent as he finished the painful crawl. His arm and back muscles burned as he maneuvered into an awkward position where he was still out of sight but could see the girl in her chair and the body of the dead guard on the floor.

But Kusnetsov was nowhere to be seen.

Quinn could see most of the green-lit warehouse, except for the front entrance and the corners. Was Kusnetsov crouching in one of those corners, texting for reinforcements?

He didn't see the telltale orange heat signature coming from any of them.

His heart hammered his breastbone as precious seconds ticked by. Winds whipped at his face. This was a hell of a time for a standoff. Why hadn't Kusnetsov fired? Was he low on bullets?

The chronograph read fifty-eight minutes left. Time was running out. Quinn leaned farther into the skylight opening so he could see the entrance.

The warehouse stayed silent.

Beyond the girl and the dead guard, he could see the front door a few inches ajar, its frame bent from the blast. If Kusnetsov had escaped, the door would be opened farther, and Quinn would have heard the sound of running footsteps.

He's still in the freaking building.

The thermal images were fuzzy, and the dead guard had a blurry outline of ghostlike orange light around his body. His heavy-set body lay on its side, the AK-47 rifle lying against its gut. Cold winds swirled in from the open door and skylight. As the warmth of the guard's body decreased, the orange thermal image faded as well.

But the orange outline at the top side of the guard's body seemed a brighter orange than the rest of the body.

There.

Something small and bright orange snaked across the guard's torso. Blood?

No. It was a human hand.

Quinn shifted his rifle into position.

You're a wily son of a bitch, Kusnetsov. He must've seen

Quinn's goggles, and was hiding in the one safe place: beneath the propped-up body of the dead guard.

And if Kusnetsov got hold of the guard's AK-47, he could blast Quinn off of the roof.

Kusnetsov's bright orange hand reached for the AK-47's pistol grip. Quinn leaned into the skylight opening and fired three rounds directly at the hand.

A shriek came from behind the guard's body, the hand jerked up, and then the guard's body rolled forward onto its stomach, exposing Kusnetsov's upper torso.

Quinn fired three shots at Kusnetsov's head and three into his chest. Orange bits and mist burst into the air, and Kusnetsov collapsed next to the dead guard.

The two bodies lay still. To a casual observer, they may have appeared asleep, except that fragments of Kusnetsov's brain lay splattered across the floor, and blood pooled from his chest onto the guard's corpse.

Quinn took a breath and removed the fusion goggles. He brushed bits of shattered glass off his phone and put it back in his pocket. From his backpack, he removed a steel carabiner, shaped like a figure eight with a larger loop at one end, and clipped the bigger loop to his webbed belt. Icy winds nipped at his fingers as he reached over to the coiled rope, secured the rope to the carabiner, and clipped the small loop to his belt.

He knocked out a remaining piece of skylight glass with his boot, perched on the edge, and rappelled down onto the warehouse floor. In seconds, his boots touched the floor, and he released the rope.

The woman watched, wide-eyed, as he walked over, his boots crunching in the broken glass. He cut the zip-ties binding her wrists and feet to the chair and removed her gag. Next, he produced a bottle of water from his backpack and handed it to her as he crouched in front of her, smiled, and spoke.

"*Ta sirs skaists vakars.*"

"*Kad nau lietus.*" Her voice came out as a croak, and she gratefully drank from the bottle of water. "And I speak English."

"Karina Lusis?" He punched buttons on his cell phone.

She nodded and took another drink of water. "American?"

"Yes, ma'am. Here to get you out."

"How?"

"A car is on its way to pick us up. Are you okay? Did they harm you?" He pulled her blouse back up over her shoulders and helped her stand.

"They slapped me a few times and made obscene threats about what they were going to do, the pigs. But I am unharmed. I've been kept sitting here. They were waiting for some sort of message. Permission, I think, from their superiors."

He was prepared for her to be paralyzed with fear or on the edge of hysteria. Instead, she seemed alert and quick-witted. She rubbed her arms to restore circulation and looked with disgust at the carnage on the floor.

Quinn's phone vibrated with the text message that the car was waiting by the side of the building.

She looked up at the hole in the ceiling where the skylight used to be. "How—"

"Come with me. I'll explain in the car."

ANTON EXPERTLY USED DARK SIDE STREETS TO TAKE THEM back into the city. Only when they crossed a major intersection did they get a glimpse, blocks away, of the bright lights and bustling crowds of the tourist areas.

They sat in the back seat. Quinn introduced himself and gave Karina a need-to-know explanation of who he was and the safe house where they were headed.

She listened intently, drinking from the bottle of water. In the shadowy light, she looked pale, thin, and wary, just like her photo. He watched for signs of shock, but her speech and body language showed her to be alert and composed.

"And what is plan after safe house, Mr. Michael Quinn?"

"We're going to get you home to Latvia."

"How? We are in Russia. The police will be looking everywhere for us. There will be roadblocks, helicopters." Her gray eyes flashed concern.

Quinn glanced at the city lights as they passed an intersection. She was right, of course. All hell would break loose as soon as Kusnetsov failed to check in. But Quinn had to keep her calm.

He explained, in a matter-of-fact tone, about the fake passports and papers, the evening clothes waiting for them at the safe house, and the cruise ship that was soon departing from St. Petersburg and headed to Latvia.

Her eyes widened as he spoke.

He ended lamely with, "So you see, all you have to do is memorize your name on your passport, and stay with me."

The Mercedes rounded a corner and pulled into the dark

cul-de-sac with the safe house. Karina looked out the window as they pulled into the driveway and then fired off a burst of anxious Latvian at the driver.

Anton responded with his own torrent of agitated Latvian, and, as he waited while the garage door opened, threw his arms in the air in a what-can-I-do gesture. After Anton finished, Karina looked at Quinn.

"This driver says all he knows is that you are highly regarded in your profession and that you know what you are doing." The garage door closed behind their car. "But to me, it seems, still great risk. You are sure this is best way?"

"Yes. Let's go upstairs, get changed, and get to our ship. You have a formal evening to attend."

THE BLACK MERCEDES SEDAN LOOKED COMMONPLACE AS it pulled in among the Bentleys, Rolls-Royces, and limousines double-parked next to the dock. Passengers from several luxury cruise ships were returning from their evening out, and the crowds mingled happily as they waited to board, drinking cocktails and chatting about the theater and the sights they had seen.

Some in the crowd might have wondered about the high-profile police presence. A line of police cars, their light bars flashing blue and red, sat parked in the center of the dock. Previous visitors to St. Petersburg may have been curious why the dock itself was now so brightly lit and why so many uniformed policemen wandered about.

And how odd that policemen were questioning the occupants of the pleasure and fishing boats in the marina, even searching the vessels. Perhaps someone's jewelry had been stolen?

No one in the milling crowd seemed to notice the young couple that emerged from the back of the Mercedes. The man in the white summer tux and the woman in the black evening gown blended in with the hundreds of similarly dressed couples about to board their ship.

Quinn's jaw tightened as he scrutinized the police presence. He glanced at his chronograph. Eighteen minutes left until the ship departed. Ordinarily, it would've been enough time, but what kind of delay would this dragnet bring?

Karina stood next to him in the chilly night air. He took her hand as the Mercedes drove off. "You're doing fine. This won't take long. All you have to do is smile and remember that you're Mrs. Jessica Ridgeway."

"Of course. Jessica Ridgeway. Jessica Ridgeway." She pronounced each syllable calmly, but her hand gripped his as they made their way through the crowd.

Quinn's heart rate quickened when he saw the two uniformed Russian Federation immigration officers, a man and a woman, standing behind a tall counter that blocked the only entrance to the *Sea Goddess*.

The boarding process had slowed to a crawl at the chokepoint, as the two officials scrutinized each passenger's passport, checking it against a computer whose monitor rested on a lower shelf hidden from public view.

They got into line behind a dozen other couples. Ahead of them, someone muttered, "My ship ID won't work here?"

A calm female voice replied, "Don't worry, dear. I brought our passports."

Quinn strained to hear what the immigration officials were saying and made out the male immigration officer repeating, "Next, please. You are leaving Russian Federation. Passport, please."

The minutes inching forward in line seemed like hours. Finally, there were just two couples ahead of them. The first, a young couple with a blissful newlywed look, smiled as they walked up and handed their passports to the Russian officials. The next couple, an elderly, white-haired man and his white-haired wife, waited patiently behind a rope and stanchions.

Quinn glanced at his chronograph. Nine minutes until the ship left. They were cutting it close, but all they had to do now was get past this checkpoint.

He broke out into a cold sweat when he looked up and noticed the two small cameras mounted on each side of the white awning above the immigration counter. But there was no avoiding them, especially now. They pointed directly at everyone who passed in front of the counter.

What if those cameras have some sort of facial recognition software?

He glanced at Karina. She'd done a good job with her makeup, given the limited time allotted. Nothing could be done about her facial features, of course. But even if the cameras did have facial recognition software, it couldn't process the image that quickly, within a couple of minutes.

Could it?

He looked back at the lights of St. Petersburg. Should they

turn around, slip out of the crowd and get back to the safe house?

No. There was no escape now. His plan would work. They had their passports, phony as they were. He gave Karina a reassuring smile.

The newlywed couple boarded the ship, holding hands. Now only the elderly couple stood ahead of them. The kindly looking white-haired man and his white-haired wife, surely of many years, walked up to the counter and handed over their passports.

Quinn's mouth felt dry and a curious hollowness filled his chest. Suppose they were caught? Neither he nor Karina would ever leave Russia alive. They would never live a long, peaceful life like that sensible white-haired couple. And all because of some wild scheme he'd dreamed up in a Berlin bar. Hiding in plain sight on a cruise ship!

They should've gone to ground. Gone off the grid entirely. The border between Russia and Latvia was mostly forest. They could've backpacked deep into the forest, and days later quietly crossed the border into Latvia. Now it was too late for that. What had he done?

"Next, please. You are leaving Russian Federation. Passport, please."

Quinn looked up, startled to see the male Russian immigration official waving him forward. The elderly couple was already halfway up the boarding ramp.

Karina's hand squeezed his as they walked up to the counter. He stitched a bland smile on his face and handed over their passports.

The male Russian officer handed Karina's passport to the

female officer. The male officer stared insolently at Quinn, then scrutinized his passport. He punched keys on his keyboard and looked at his hidden monitor.

Quinn glanced at the female officer. She was doing the same routine with Karina.

Both officers stared silently at their screens.

The male officer looked up. "Did you enjoy your evening, Mr. Ridgeway?"

"Yes, very much." Quinn wiped his sweaty free hand on his pants.

"And you, Mrs. Ridgeway?" spoke the female Russian officer, staring at Karina.

"Ye-Yes." Karina stammered. Her fingers tightened around Quinn's.

There was silence while the female officer gave Karina a sharp glance, then looked at her monitor. Was she waiting for Karina to say something more, to smoke her out? Quinn should've coached her on this. Would Karina freeze up if the officer asked her where she'd been that evening?

The bizarre idea flashed through Quinn's mind of leaping over the counter, taking out both officers…

"Forgive me for staring, Mrs. Ridgeway," spoke the female officer. "I was admiring your beautiful gown. Please visit Russia again. *Do svidaniya.*"

"*Do svidaniya,*" replied Karina as the officers handed both passports back to them.

Without looking back, Quinn led Karina up the entrance ramp and aboard the great ship. The engines throbbed beneath them.

At the top of the ramp, a foyer with a curving staircase in

the middle led off in three directions to hallways. To their left, music played through the open double doors of the ballroom. The music sounded friendly, so Quinn led Karina into the large, dome-ceilinged room.

Before them played a scene that could've been a grand supper club from an old Hollywood movie. In the middle of the room, a tuxedo-clad band, complete with a conductor, played a waltz. Couples swirled happily on a parquet dance floor.

To the right stood a lavish buffet table, ready for the after-theater, late-dinner crowd. An ice sculpture of a ballerina graced the center of the table, surrounded by platters loaded with crab, shrimp, lobster, and appetizers. Laughter and greetings filled the air as couples gathered around the buffet.

It all seemed beamed in from a better place, far from the killing field at the warehouse.

"I don't know how your body clock is doing, Karina, but I imagine you're hungry."

"Very much so. I have had nothing but crackers and water. But I do not like crowds. We can eat somewhere where is quiet?" The red vinyl booths behind the band were already filling with boisterous couples, and passengers had formed a line up at the bar. Karina, intimidated by the scene, moved so close to Quinn that she touched him.

"Of course." He led her to the back of the ballroom, to a secluded area of tables, and selected a table for two next to a window that overlooked the sea.

As they sat down, he heard the clanking and grinding noises of the ramp pulling up followed by the rumble of the ship's engines revving.

Several blue-and-white police boats, their light bars flashing, drifted in the water outside their window. Men on the deck of one boat shouted and waved their arms at men on the deck of another. A third police boat gave a short blast from its horn.

The *Sea Goddess* sounded its own sonorous, low-pitched horn as it slowly pulled away from the dock. They were on their way.

A waiter appeared, lit the candles, and took their drink orders. Quinn ordered a Glenfiddich on the rocks, Karina a vodka tonic. After the waiter left, Quinn smiled and glanced at Karina, looking for signs of shock or post-traumatic stress.

The opposite seemed to be taking place. As Karina looked around the great room, taking in the crystal chandeliers, the polished silver glinting on candle-lit tables, and the liveried waiters speaking in hushed tones, the white-knuckled tension she had shown at the dock seemed to melt away.

She was becoming more comfortable with her surroundings. Away from the crowds, absorbing the cheerful elegance all around, her body language relaxed and her eyes shone with curiosity.

When the waiter returned with their drinks, the *Sea Goddess* had picked up speed and cruised past the harbor. Quinn made small talk as they sipped their drinks and watched the lights of the police boats and St. Petersburg recede in the distance. Surprised by her resilience, he finally concluded that, for a small country, Latvia produced operatives of the highest quality.

When the golden lights of the city vanished into the horizon, she folded her hands on the table and looked at him as if seeing him for the first time.

"I must confess, Mr. Quinn, I had doubts about wisdom of your plan. But you have shown you are highly capable." She sipped her drink. "Is hard to believe this is real. But here we are. And are we now—"

She startled as the piercing shrieks of police sirens cut her off mid-sentence. A small fishing boat with its lights turned off sped by their window, parallel with the *Sea Goddess*. Behind it, four of the blue-and-white police boats gave close chase in formation, their light bars flashing.

The fishing boat shot past the *Sea Goddess*, its white wake frothing high in the lights of the police boats. About fifty yards past the bow of the cruise ship, the fishing boat abruptly made a splashy U-turn and then stopped, dead in the water, facing its pursuers.

The police boats quickly surrounded it on all sides, and men on the decks threw grappling hooks onto the rails of the fishing boat.

"What is that all about?" Karina watched the policemen climb onto the fishing boat as the vessels floated by.

"I believe that a woman fitting your description was reported as boarding that fishing boat. But when the police search that boat, all they'll find is a drunken old Russian fisherman who has forgotten to turn on his running lights."

She sighed as she watched the bobbing police boats recede behind the *Goddess*. "You are person who thinks of everything."

"Not everything. But I believe you were going to ask if we are finally safe?"

"I was." She turned away from the window and faced him, eyebrows raised.

"That point where the fishing boat turned around was the end of the twelve-mile nautical limit that is considered Russian territory. We are now in international waters and beyond the reach of the Russian Federation." Quinn raised his whiskey glass. "So yes, Karina, we are now safe."

For the first time since he'd met her, her lips curved up in a smile. It was the hopeful smile of someone who has completed a dark journey, but now turned the corner into the sunlight, and was ready to enjoy life. She touched her glass to his, her eyes bright with excitement.

He smiled back but suddenly was bone-tired. The adrenaline that had fueled him all night faded as his body grudgingly acknowledged the "mission accomplished" signal sent from his brain. He finished his whiskey. Its fire would keep him going down the home stretch.

Karina sipped her vodka tonic and flipped through the menu. Quinn's original plan, once he had her on board, had been to sedate her and have her sleep in his cabin. That plan was now out the window.

"For someone who's been through what you have, Karina, you're certainly handling it well."

"You have not met many Latvians?"

"Well, no." He thought of the old woman on Love Lock Bridge in Riga.

"We are a reserved people, but self-sufficient. And strong." She smiled again. "We have had to be, Mr. Quinn. I may now call you Michael?"

"Of course."

Throughout the entire mission, Quinn had thought of her as shown in that grim photo in the Berlin bar. He had memorized that photo in order to recognize her, and she had looked much the same in the warehouse. Even after her makeover in the safe house, he'd only had time to check that her appearance matched the doctored passport photo. His impression was of an efficient but cold operative, married to her work.

Now he couldn't help but notice how attractive her long brown hair looked, worn straight down in back against her bare white shoulders. Curving, high cheekbones gave her face a delicate prettiness. Up close, her fair skin was soft and smooth, and her generous lips had just the right touch of lipstick.

And those eyes. They were, he decided, a soft dove-gray with blue highlights. Even in that Berlin photo, they had been striking. Now they were strikingly beautiful.

In fact, she was beautiful anyplace he looked.

She finished her drink and set her glass on the table. "What happens next?"

"You must be tired, even if you don't feel it. After dinner, you should get some rest. Your supervisor, Helena, packed some clothes and personal items for you. I have a pretty nice suite with a separate living room and a couch that converts to a bed. I'll take the couch, and you get the master bedroom. Tomorrow morning, we dock in Riga."

Karina sat back in her chair and crossed her legs. A slit up the side of her dress showed a tantalizing glimpse of well-toned thigh. Her slim figure seemed made for the form-fitting black gown.

Outside their window, stars gleamed across a pristine black

sky. The sea was calm and quiet, as if it had always been so. Moonlight shimmered on a streak of rippling water.

In the ballroom area behind them, things had quieted down from the boisterous beginning. The band was playing a slow-dance ballad.

"I will do as you say, Michael. But I may make one request?"

"Certainly."

"Can we dance?"

"What?" He straightened up, not sure if he had heard correctly.

"Just one dance, please? I will explain."

"I'd be delighted." He pushed his chair back. *Why the hell not?*

Quinn led her onto the dance floor. The lights were dimmed, and the atmosphere had segued into a late-evening intimacy. The band ended its song, and couples waited quietly for the music to start again.

He held her in dance position as they waited for the music. Sitting at the table, he had only been able to look at her. Now he could feel her and, as he inhaled the enticing aroma of her perfume and perspiration, almost taste her. Her mouth, lips slightly parted, lingered only inches away. Slender eyebrows arched gracefully over eyes that looked at him with unconcealed interest.

His fatigue disappeared, replaced by stimulation from the whiskey and from the girl in his arms.

"Karina, you were going to explain?"

"Of course." He felt her breath on his face as she spoke. "How to say? Michael, we are from different worlds. In United

States, in your profession, I'm sure you are used to all this." She glanced around the room, and when she looked back, her eyes glistened.

"Where I grew up, we saw scenes like this only in movies. I lived in crowded apartment where heat was turned off every April. I waited in breadlines, lines for everything, and always there were shortages. Most of time we had cold water only, so we had to go to communal baths to shower.

"Something like this, so beautiful, is like Cinderella. It is unlikely I experience anything like this again. So this dance means much to me."

Quinn was about to reply when a low rumbling noise came from somewhere behind the ship. The band started into another slow ballad but stopped after a few bars as the rumbling quickly grew louder, drowning out all other sounds.

The dancing couples looked around, confused. The noise was way too loud to be anything from the ship's engines. Silverware jangled, and glasses vibrated on tables. The great chandeliers above them swayed, and their crystal prisms clinked.

The sound quickly escalated to a roar. Gasps came from the crowd as they not only heard the noise but *felt* it, hammering their eardrums and vibrating their bones. The air itself seemed to shake.

The roar rose to a grating screech, the kind that preceded an explosion. It sounded like a missile, coming right at them. Dancers covered their ears. Quinn wrapped his arms around a trembling Karina and pulled her close.

Shouts and cries rang across the ballroom as a *boom*, like a massive thunderclap, sounded directly overhead. The entire ship shuddered, caught in an invisible undertow as the pressure wave of air washed over the ship like a tsunami. Wine glasses rolled off tables and crashed to the floor.

The thunder rolled over the ship and kept going, fading as it traveled farther away, finally vanishing somewhere in the distant night sky.

For a moment, no one moved. Then busboys ran out to sweep up the broken glass, and waiters appeared with new bottles of wine. The band resumed playing, and the crowd buzzed about the strange noise.

"What was that?" Karina looked at him with wide eyes.

"A Russian SU-24 fighter jet, buzzing us at a very low height and at a very high speed."

"Why?"

Quinn was silent for a moment. *The cameras back at the dock did have facial recognition software. But the software had identified her too late.*

There was no need to explain this. The mission was over.

"Just sour grapes from the loser, Karina. We've won this battle."

Her bare back was damp where his hand held her. She was still in his embrace, her body just touching his.

He caressed her cheek. "Now, about that dance."

TEXAS TIME

A MICHAEL QUINN SHORT STORY

KEVIN SCOTT OLSON

Let him who desires peace prepare for war.

— FLAVIUS

TEXAS TIME

Tamaulipas, Mexico

IN THE COPPER GLOW OF SUNSET, THE MEXICAN DESERT seemed to know something was about to happen.

Long shadows of night crept across the rolling badlands. Restless winds tossed fistfuls of sand at scrawny mesquite shrubs.

Hunkered down in his shallow foxhole, Michael Quinn scratched his three-day growth of beard and spat sand out of his mouth. Even with his camo netting, wind-driven sand still got in his face and tried to gum up his equipment.

He picked up his binoculars and focused them on his target.

The six semi-trailers, each one forty feet long, stood side-by-side in the sand a few hundred yards away. Three Mexican men, dressed in fatigues and army boots, sat in folding chairs and guarded the trailers. The men talked and drank out of brown bottles. Their AK-47 rifles lay carelessly on the ground next to their chairs.

Encroaching shadows now covered the last of the trailers. The evening's first stars twinkled in the darkening sky. Quinn tested the strap of his backpack and checked the round in the chamber of his HK 9mm again.

Almost time.

One of the Mexican guards stood and stretched. A second guard lit a cigarette, stood, and motioned to the third. The three guards picked up their rifles, chatted some more, then turned and casually walked away from the trailers, laughing and joking, carrying their rifles almost as an afterthought.

Quinn bit his lower lip. The *Escorpiones* might be the most brutal drug cartel in Mexico, but they sorely lacked in military discipline.

And that weakness was their soft underbelly.

He watched through his binoculars as the guards walked away from him and over a sandy knoll, heading to the ramshackle cantina a few hundred yards past the trailers. The humble building with the corrugated tin roof was where the guards went to have their dinner and drink their fill. Light spilled out from a bright interior as the guards entered the cantina, and then the double doors closed behind them.

Go.

Moving fast and keeping low to the ground, Quinn scrambled out of his foxhole and across the low desert hills. In seconds, he reached the first trailer. He removed his backpack, crawled underneath the trailer, and rolled onto his back. The trailer wheels had been removed to prevent theft, and the trailers stood on blocks instead.

His SEALs demolitions training served him well. In forty minutes, the innocent-looking bricks of C4 explosive from his backpack were molded like modeling clay in the recessed areas underneath the trailers, near the wheelbases.

In order to find them, someone would have to crawl underneath in the dirt and darkness, and even then, they'd have to know where to look. Quinn set the timers and detonators for midnight, Texas time.

He grunted as he rolled out from underneath the last trailer. Wiping the sweat off his face, he crouched in the darkness and looked around. Nothing but sand and mesquite and the cold desert wind. Above him, stars shone silently in a coal-black sky.

Five hours later
The Longhorn Lounge
Dallas, Texas

OF ALL THE SENSUAL DELIGHTS MAN HAS TREASURED over the centuries, surely one of the finest combinations must be Glenfiddich single-malt whiskey on the rocks and warm female companionship.

They went together in so many ways.

The first taste of Quinn's second whiskey had already started its slow burn, and the oaken taste lingered. And Samantha, the lovely Southern belle serving him tonight, lingered as well. She stood so close that he breathed in her peach scent, probably from the body wash she'd showered with that morning.

She leaned forward and placed a fresh napkin under his glass of whiskey. Her long blonde hair brushed his arm as she spoke in her soft Texas murmur. "And how's that second one workin' for ya?"

"Samantha, it's perfect. Now that we've met, I'm going to come here every night from now on and drink good whiskey with you."

"Oh, really? And how long are you staying here at the Renaissance?"

"Well, just the night. But I can come back."

"We'll just see about that." She smiled. "In the meantime, how about a bite to eat? Kitchen's closing pretty soon."

"You read my mind. Man can't live on drink alone. It's been a long day." He looked at the menu she handed him. His last meal had been ten hours earlier—a miserable MRE in the desert.

"Let's go with eggs, scrambled light. Bacon, crisp. Your homemade buttermilk biscuits. And another whiskey."

Samantha sat down in the leather chair across from him. She crossed her legs, and the definition from her muscle tone showed through the white jersey dress. Her blue eyes sparkled with amusement.

"Bacon and eggs and whiskey," she said.

"That does seem a bit odd. Okay, put the whiskey in a cup of black coffee."

"Yes, sir." She giggled. "I'll put the order in and be back soon."

Quinn watched her walk away. All of the waitresses in the

bar wore white, clinging jersey dresses with a discreet slit up one side. With her fair skin and her tall, athletic build, Samantha wore hers with elegance. They'd chatted and flirted all through his first drink. She was a native Texan, a runner, twenty-four, and was putting herself through law school.

He sat back in his chair and looked around the room. The Longhorn was a lounge and restaurant that occupied half of the top floor of the Grand Renaissance hotel near the Dallas airport. Tobacco-brown leather chairs and gray granite tables furnished its interior.

Late on a Monday night, only a few scattered groups of businessmen patronized the Longhorn, conversing and putting the finishing touches on their long day. Above the bar, television screens silently displayed sports and business channels. The picture windows on three sides showed the starry night and the lights of a prosperous city.

The tablet screen sitting next to his drink showed the day's results from the world's stock markets. He tapped an icon, and the picture changed to what he was really watching—an encrypted satellite view of the patch of Mexican desert where he'd lived the past few days.

The six trailers stood side-by-side, bathed in the pale moonlight. The three Mexican guards were back in their folding chairs, guarding the trailers. One of them chewed on a toothpick. Another one yawned and patted his belly.

Quinn scrolled the picture to the right.

Past a sandy knoll, a few hundred yards over from the trailers, sat the cantina where the guards had gone for dinner. From the aerial view, the building sat in the middle of nowhere, surrounded only by sand and rocks. A solitary road led out of its gravel parking lot. The pickup trucks and old cars of the cantina's patrons sat in the parking lot.

Quinn flicked the picture back to the world markets and looked at his watch. 11:40 p.m. Twenty minutes to show time.

Time for a phone call. And this call had to be done right.

Samantha was across the room waiting on a table. He stood up, caught her eye, and motioned that he would be back. Then he picked up his tablet, walked out of the Longhorn bar, and down the hall.

The logistics of the mission had been his call. The trailers contained a massive cache of stolen weapons. The *Escorpiones*, one of the Mexican drug cartels warring south of the Texas border, had somehow obtained the weapons from a warehouse on an American military base.

How the cartel had infiltrated the military, along with accomplishing such a brazen theft, was intel classified beyond Quinn's level.

But the intel that he'd seen—that among the missing arms were huge quantities of light anti-tank rockets, rocket-propelled grenades, and hundreds of thousands of rounds of ammunition—would have alone been enough to raise concern at high levels.

The men's room was at the end of the hall. Inside, it was well-appointed as well as blessedly empty. At the gray granite counter, he splashed his face with cold water and looked in the mirror.

The man in the mirror, in his sport coat, open-collared shirt, and slacks, resembled the sort of early-thirties Dallas businessman one might see at the Longhorn.

His medium-brown hair was parted on the side in a traditional business-casual style, and his blue-gray eyes hid their intensity behind a calm demeanor. The five o'clock shadow on his lean jawline fit the look, given the late hour, and his sun-bronzed skin could be from any number of outdoor sports.

Nothing indicated that the man in sport coat and slacks had spent the last three days sweltering in camouflage clothes in the Mexican desert, running an op against the *Escorpiones* drug cartel.

That cartel had already taken over another border town and now wanted to conquer the entire Mexican state of Tamaulipas. Such bold ambition required arms befitting a well-equipped military, not merely a gang. If they pulled off this theft, they would have the arms they needed. The concern now would no longer be chaos at the border, but the possible collapse of Mexico itself.

"The United States does not need a Somalia next door," the Director had warned at Quinn's briefing.

The US military couldn't cross the border. Attempting to deal with the corrupt Mexican government would only play into the hands of the cartels. Covert action was called for, and by operatives not concerned with the niceties of legal jurisdiction in an area that was a failed state run by warlords.

A few days ago, US intelligence had located the trailers hiding the arms and munitions.

And Quinn had been sent there to neutralize the problem.

His watch flashed that it was 11:45.

He locked himself in a stall, pulled out a disposable cell phone, and dialed a Mexican number. A loud voice answered the phone on the first ring.

Quinn whispered in harsh Spanish, "*There's a bomb under-*

neath your pigsty of a bar. Everyone within a quarter mile has five minutes to get away. This is the only phone call you'll receive. Viva El Sangre!"

He turned off the cell phone and removed the SD card and battery. He snapped the SD card in two, flushed the card and battery down the toilet, and exited the stall. After dropping the cell phone into the trash, he exited the men's room and walked back down the empty hallway.

As he walked, he tapped his tablet screen to show the scene in the Mexican desert.

The three guards now stood, brandishing their rifles and looking with alarm at something to their right. Quinn scrolled the picture over.

People clambered out of the cantina, tossing their drinks and cigarettes on the gravel. They piled into their trucks and cars and sped down the blacktop road. In minutes the cantina had emptied, and only an old Chevy sedan remained in the gravel parking lot.

The cantina had received his message.

The three Mexicans guards ran into view from the left side of the screen, still carrying their rifles, and one of them held a cell phone to his ear. They stopped in the cantina's parking lot and looked around. The guards piled into the sedan and fled.

His phone call had worked. They'd taken the threat of a bomb placed by a rival cartel seriously. The empty cantina stared back at him.

He walked back into the Longhorn. There were only a few customers left, and the lounge was quiet.

He sat down at his table, propped the tablet on its stand in front of him, and sipped his whiskey-coffee. Instead of feeling anxious, he felt an inner calm. His card had been played. There was nothing more for him to do but wait for the big bang.

The mouth-watering aroma of bacon and eggs wafted over from his left. Samantha appeared with the tray of food. She laid the plates on the granite table and glanced at Quinn, as if deciding something, then walked away.

The scrambled eggs had just the right consistency, the biscuits were fresh-baked, and the bacon was maple-cured—nectar from the gods. It had been days since he'd eaten real food.

As he buttered the last biscuit, Samantha reappeared and sat down in the chair across from him, holding a chilled glass of white wine.

"Break time?" Quinn moved his tablet so that its back faced her and only he could see the screen.

"Done time," she said. "My shift ends at midnight. They let me off a few minutes early. I stayed to make sure you got your food."

"Then let's toast the end of the day for both of us." His whiskey-coffee cup clinked against her wine glass, and they drank.

She sat back in her chair and stretched out her exquisite legs, crossing them at the ankles.

Quinn studied her lithe figure. He imagined her in running shorts and a sports bra, on a sunny day somewhere in the countryside, sprinting with the effortless grace of a gazelle.

A soft blue light flashed from his watch. Eleven fifty-five. Five minutes until the big bang in the desert.

Random thoughts crossed his mind. Should he have done

it differently? And how—walk across the desert to take on three armed men? Stay to watch the explosion and risk being caught in a dragnet?

Suppose the guards had found the explosives and disarmed them? Or suppose the detonators malfunctioned? Then, in a few minutes, nothing would happen. In an hour or so, everyone would return to the cantina, have a beer, and laugh about the prank phone call that had caused the needless evacuation.

He banished the thoughts and sipped his whiskey-coffee.

"So, Samantha, you're a runner. I'm guessing you like to run long?"

"More than just about anything. The area where I grew up in Texas was made for long-distance running. All ranch land. Folks there said it was so flat you could watch your dog run away from you for three days."

"I can imagine. What got you into long-distance?"

"It was an escape from reality, I guess." Samantha glanced out the window at the stars. "Not the greatest childhood. Running was a way to leave my cares behind."

"I see."

"Things worked out okay, though. I made captain of my high school cross-country team. A track scholarship helped pay for my college undergrad. These days, to burn off the stress of work and law school, I run marathons. Two, three a year."

"You must like it when the 'runner's high' kicks in."

"I so do! There's nothing like it. Yeah, the pain melts away, and you feel invincible. But there's more; you also lose all sense of time. That's the incredible part. It feels like you could just go forever."

Quinn thought for a moment. "You work long hours here and have law school full-time. Throw in all those hours training for marathons. You've got a pretty busy life."

"I schedule almost every part of my day. I have one of those apps that organizes your life into fifteen-minute segments. It's the only way I get everything done." She looked down at her drink. "Stressful, some say. Then again, most everyone I meet —here at the Longhorn, or at school—is stressed. They're all trapped by their schedules. Everyone I know has their life dictated by having to get something done by a certain time."

The soft blue light on Quinn's watch flashed that it was 11:58 p.m. Two minutes until the big bang. His heart rate picked up as he thought of the detonator timers, hidden in the Mexican desert.

Samantha looked tired but happy. The long day was catching up with her. Even so, her blue eyes still twinkled as she looked at him. "People are so darn busy that they don't realize that the present moment is also the best moment."

"Why is that?"

"Because it's never going to occur again."

Samantha leaned forward. The ends of her blonde hair touched her knees, and her eyes looked into his. "Have you ever wished you could, just once in a while, make time stand still?"

The soft blue light on Quinn's watch flashed that it was 11:59 p.m. "Can you hold that thought? I need to check on something. Won't take long."

"Of course." Samantha watched with curiosity as he picked up the tablet and held it on his lap, tilting it towards him so only his eyes could see the screen.

He touched the screen and zoomed in on the trailers.

Ten seconds. He drank again from his whiskey-coffee and let the fire burn in his belly.

Five.

Four.

Three.

Two.

One.

The soft blue light on Quinn's watch flashed that it was 12:00 a.m.

Midnight.

Nothing happened.

Ten seconds late. Fifteen. The seconds ticking by seemed an eternity. Quinn felt cold sweat on the back of his neck. He had dual-primed the detonators. Had he double-checked the timers?

Movement on the tablet screen caught his eye. It lit up with what looked like a series of solar flares. Then the screen went completely white.

Quinn zoomed back out. Six separate explosions slowly morphed into a gigantic yellow fireball, floating up into a massive mushroom cloud.

Brilliant white streaks shot out of the sides of the fireball, firing in all directions. Some flew in a straight line into the night, others flared out in short arcs and then exploded in violent bursts. The munitions. The hundreds of thousands of rounds of ammunition, the anti-tank rockets, the rocket-propelled grenades.

Quinn touched the screen, and the picture flicked back to the world stock-markets, showing the mid-day returns from Asia.

"Samantha, please excuse me, I need to send a quick text." He took out his actual cell phone and typed the encrypted text he'd been waiting to send: *Prometheus.*

The code word that meant, for this operation only, "mission accomplished."

Seconds later, the phone vibrated with the return text: *Poseidon.*

His message had been received and conveyed to the Director.

"Some late-night business, Michael?" Samantha asked.

"Yes, thanks for understanding. All done." Quinn looked out the windows at the city lights. "You're right, you know."

"About what?"

"That the present moment is the best moment."

Her voice was a soft murmur. "And what should we do about that?"

Quinn's phone vibrated as another text came in: *Your 8 a.m. flight has been changed to the first flight out, leaving at 5:45 a.m. New business. Confirm.*

He texted his acknowledgment, wondering what "new business" might mean.

He looked up at Samantha. "It turns out I have to leave in a few hours to catch a plane."

Her fingers caressed her wine glass, drawing little circles on the frosted outside. "That's too bad. I was hoping we'd have some time get to know each other better. Y'know, make that ol' world stop awhile? Make time stand still?"

Quinn sat back in his chair. Outside, a golden moon watched over a peaceful, starry sky. The world seemed, if only for a while, a better place.

He glanced at his cell phone, then did something he was never supposed to do.

He turned it off.

Quinn watched the phone screen slowly go dark. For good measure, he took off his watch and put them both in his pocket.

He smiled at Samantha. "Consider it done."

ROSEBLOOD

A Michael Quinn Short Story

Kevin Scott Olson

Desire is stronger than compulsion.

— RUSSIAN PROVERB

ROSEBLOOD

Friday evening
Kronberg Concert Hall
New York City, New York

VIEWED THROUGH THE CRYSTAL-CLEAR ILLUMINATION OF Michael Quinn's riflescope, the young woman played the piano as if she were making love.

During quiet passages, her body swayed from side to side as her fingers caressed the keys. As the tempo increased and the intensity built, she rocked back and forth in a passionate embrace of the music, her long blonde hair falling down her back.

From his sniper's nest in the cramped electrical room, high above and in front of the stage, Quinn peered through the riflescope and scanned the stage around the girl.

Who would want to harm her?

Absorbed in an intense *presto* passage, the girl leaned in, her face almost touching the keys. The fingers of her right hand blurred up and down the keyboard while her left hand anchored the movement with a pounding rhythm. The plangent notes of the solitary piano filled the high-ceilinged concert hall with as much power and fury as a full orchestra.

The electrical room, which was little more than a large closet, made for a good overwatch position but was unventilated and warm. Quinn's shirt collar stuck to the back of his neck, and clammy pools itched under his arms.

The small of his back ached from sitting on the stepladder, his makeshift perch. He removed a bandana from his back pocket, wiped away the beads of sweat gathered at the top of his forehead, then glanced down at the damp, faded blue cotton in his hand.

No, it didn't go with the rest of his attire for an evening at a concert hall. But he was loyal to that bandana. It had served him in barren deserts and on bitterly cold mountains. It would serve him here. With a dry section of the fabric, he wiped off the ring of perspiration on the rubber eyepiece and tucked the bandana back in his pocket.

Sliding the small, rectangular window open another couple of inches, he moved the rifle barrel, making sure the entire concert hall was within range. Then he leaned forward and resumed his surveillance.

The *presto* movement ended, and a pause hushed the concert hall, like the eerie silence after passing thunder. The music continued but softened to an *adagio*. Restful notes wafted into the waiting air.

The girl's fingers shifted into slow motion, lingering as long as possible on each key. She leaned back, and the spotlight framed her upturned face. The girl's eyes closed and opened as if the light had triggered some brief, private ecstasy.

She's "Sleeping Beauty," Quinn decided. But one whose eyes were to be closed for only a few seconds, not a hundred years. The scope's magnification confirmed his belief that some women were born beautiful, and this girl was one of those.

Her flawless white skin was luminous in the spotlight, and the honey-blonde hair had a natural luster. With her fair coloring, she probably hailed from the northern part of Russia.

She wore little eye makeup and didn't need to; her dark-brown eyebrows and baby-blue eyes were striking against her fair skin. The only face makeup visible through the scope was her crimson lipstick.

Dialing back the scope, he guessed her to be about five foot seven, with a figure somewhere between that of a model and a centerfold. She'd look just as hot dressed in a white T-shirt and faded blue-jean shorts as she did in tonight's black evening gown.

But, she may as well be a thousand miles away. Quinn sighed as he adjusted the scope. This assignment was to be all work and no play.

The call had come the previous morning, when Quinn was in Key West, en route home. He had flown to Virginia for the briefing, where it was made clear his anonymity as an independent contractor for the CIA made him the preferred choice for such a sensitive case, and then on to New York.

Reliable intel indicated an attempt on the girl's life might be made during her two-night engagement in New York. It was known that the Russian FSB, every bit as ruthless as its KGB predecessor, had a target painted on her pretty little back. Beyond that, however, there wasn't much to go on. The danger to her was unspecified, and there were no suspects or suspicious activities reported in the area. Current FSB techniques ran the gamut from poisoning to staged accidents, so Quinn had no choice but to look at everything in the concert hall, searching for anything out of the ordinary.

It was a solo engagement, and the stage held only the girl and her nine-foot Steinway concert grand piano, topped with a vase of red roses. Off to the sides, the assorted stagehands and technicians watched in rapt silence.

Quinn zoomed in on the latticework, battens, and cables of the catwalk. Nothing unusual. He put down his AR-10 .308 rifle, picked up his night-vision binoculars, and scanned, for the umpteenth time, the audience.

Everything looked as it had for the past two hours. The orchestra and three ascending terraces of box seats held groups of well-dressed concertgoers, mostly couples ranging from middle-aged to elderly, with a sprinkling of scruffier-dressed twenty-somethings who were probably music students.

He examined every seat on the main floor, then the high-end box seats in the terraces. By now, he knew practically every seat in the concert hall. Nothing seemed amiss or suspicious.

After three sweeps of the hall, he put down the binoculars and picked up his rifle, adjusting the scope. She was nearing the end of her encore. If anything were going to happen tonight, it would happen soon.

The girl leaned forward, concentrating as she plunged into a showy cadenza. Why did blonde-haired Russian women tend to wear their hair straight down like that? Individual rivulets of perspiration, the result of her sheer exertion on the cool, air-conditioned stage, trickled down the skin of her bare back.

Her intensity was captivating. This girl's passion in life was clearly her music. Everything else would be a distant second.

His finger gripped the trigger guard as the concert hall fell silent.

The girl still leaned forward but had lifted her hands off the piano. The cadenza had ended, and, for a few seconds, her fingers hung in the air above the keys, moving in a sort of silent ballet. Time itself seemed to stop.

Then her hands descended, pounding out loud, sonorous chords, bringing the audience home with a powerful *rondo*. Waves of music filled the hall as the last movement built toward its climax. With a victorious smile like that of an athlete crossing the finish line, she struck the final chord.

The notes faded, and the girl raised both hands off the piano in one graceful flourish. She sat erect, staring straight ahead while her hands rested demurely on her thighs.

A moment of silence hung in the air, followed by a roar as the audience stood and cheered and applauded.

The girl turned toward them with a slight hesitation, as if her sleeping-beauty spell had just been broken, and she was noticing the audience for the first time. The spotlight followed her as she stood and walked toward the front of the stage.

His nerves taut, Quinn watched the girl bow gracefully to the left, to the center, then to the right of the hall. Now, with the noise and distraction of the crowd, would be a prime window for an attack. Yet no one rushed the stage or entered the aisles.

Flashes of deep red flitted through the air, startling Quinn until he realized the people in the front rows were throwing dozens of long-stemmed red roses at the girl's feet. Right—this was a tradition at this girl's performances. Her adoring audiences showered the stage with red roses, her favorite flower.

The pianist flung her arms out in salute to her assembled court, gracious as she basked in wave after wave of applause. The volume of the cheering increased as she bowed one last time and blew kisses of farewell.

The audience kept standing, kept clapping and cheering and yelling for more.

"All clear," Quinn said into his headset microphone.

"Roger that," rasped Doyle's voice through his earpiece.

Doyle and Russo, the two blue-uniformed NYPD officers guarding the girl, emerged from the sides and escorted her offstage.

With a sigh of relief, Quinn pulled in his rifle and slid the tinted window shut. He stepped off the ladder, stretched his back and legs, and took a swig from his bottle of water.

He pulled back the charging handle and ejected the live round from the chamber. Then he unscrewed the suppressor from the barrel, removed the magazine and takedown pin, and broke down the rifle. It would be stored for the night in a metal cabinet here in the electrical room.

The stainless-steel cabinet doors had a finish as reflective as the chrome on an automobile bumper. His reflection stared back at him as he locked the cabinet. He still looked presentable. His shirt and slacks showed no outward signs of the sweat now drying on various parts of his body.

He ran a hand through his hair, with its business-casual cut matted down here and there. His eyes looked a bit tired, and his jawline showed a shadow. Could've used a second shave before going out this evening.

But this was New York in the twenty-first century. Some of the attendees in the cheap seats wore jeans and parkas. When he put his sport coat on and left the concert hall, carrying his topcoat and program, he would be, to all appearances, the thirty-something businessman his cover conveyed.

He took a last swig of water and put the bottle back on the ladder rung. One night down, and one more night to go.

Not just yet, he corrected himself. This first night wasn't quite over. He looked down at the glossy program sitting on the ladder rung next to his bottle of water.

Anna Marina Kosenko, the program proclaimed in bold type beneath a color photograph of the girl on a stage strewn with red roses. The twenty-one-year-old, Russian-born prodigy, living in London and generating excitement in performances around the globe with her astonishing virtuosity and sensual interpretations. Now appearing, for two nights only, in an exclusive engagement at the famed Kronberg Concert Hall.

No, things weren't quite over.

He was going to meet Anna Marina Kosenko, and spend the evening with her

---

One hour later
The Grand Empire Hotel, New York City

IN THE CONTROLLED CHAOS THAT IS NEW YORK CITY,

the Grand Empire Hotel was, following a period of decline, once again truly grand. Quinn had visited the hotel in its not-so-grand days to meet a contact in the less-than-reputable bar.

But now the hotel was once more a destination for the wealthy and famous and a hangout for those who hoped to become so. As the glass-walled elevator took him up to the penthouse floor, Quinn admired the handsome refurbishing of the lounge and made a mental note to try the new sushi bar.

The elevator doors opened to a quiet hallway with a polished marble floor and a coffered ceiling. Doyle and Russo stood guard outside her penthouse. They nodded as Quinn walked up.

"You ready for some babysitting?" Doyle, in his mid- to late fifties, had the scratchy voice of an ex-smoker. His eyes, though friendly, had a seen-it-all weariness. His broad shoulders and thick neck indicated a youth of weightlifting and football, but his ample belly and florid complexion indicated a man looking forward to retirement.

His partner, Russo, was a study in contrast. Thin, shorter, and probably not yet thirty, he was the type who kept quiet yet was always ready for action. His dark eyes conveyed curiosity, as if wondering what this assignment was really all about.

Need to know basis. You both know only what's necessary.

"How is the young lady?" Quinn asked.

"Fer Chrissake," replied Doyle, "you'd think having your cell phone taken away for a coupla nights was a matter of life and death. But the real tantrum came when we informed her that she couldn't go out on the town tonight." He jerked his head toward the door. "You gotcher work cut out for you in there."

"I'll order up some hot chocolate and graham crackers, and she'll be fine."

Doyle's face creased in a wide grin, and he gave Quinn a *you're-all-right* look as he rang the porcelain doorbell.

"Come in!" shouted a muffled female voice from somewhere inside the suite.

As Doyle slid his keycard into the door slot, he winked at Quinn.

"At least she's a looker. Damn! Wish I was your age." His voice lowered as the door opened. "Well, here you go. We'll be outside here until zero two hundred. Then the night shift will take over. We'll see you tomorrow night back at the concert hall. Ha! Assuming you make it through tonight."

The door closed behind Quinn with a solid double-click, and he stood alone in the foyer. Ahead of him was the living room, and to the right, a short hallway led to the bedroom. The faint sound of a running shower came from the master bath.

"Wait out there," commanded a girl's voice from the bathroom.

Quinn sat down in one of two wingback guest chairs in the foyer. With his suitcase on the floor next to him, he could've been a well-dressed salesman waiting for an appointment. He touched the HK 9mm in his shoulder holster as he looked around.

The small foyer was well appointed, with oil paintings and a cherry Queen Anne table. His attention quickly moved, however, to the striking living room. More than half of the room's far wall consisted of a large picture window, at least twenty feet wide, with a panoramic view of Times Square.

A kaleidoscope of moving auto headlights, brightly lit theater marquees, and mammoth, high-definition electronic billboards offered a view as garish as anything on the Las Vegas strip. The spectacle was muted only by the January snowfall that had turned to slush, leaving gray piles atop car rooftops and black puddles in the streets.

The thick window glass shut out the street noise, and the quiet living room offered a comfortable-looking sofa, loveseat, and chair. To the left stood a small bar with a black granite counter. To the right, behind the sofa, sat an ebony concert grand piano, on top of which a crystal vase held red roses.

As Quinn wondered how the hotel had fit the piano into the suite, he heard the sound of the bedroom door closing.

Anna Kosenko walked into the living room and turned to face him.

She was barefoot, wearing nothing but a long, luxuriously thick, white cotton bathrobe with "Grand Empire" embroidered on the left breast. Her face was scrubbed clean of makeup, and her wet hair was combed straight down in back.

She doesn't even need a T-shirt and shorts. She's gorgeous just out of the shower. He stood and offered a polite smile.

She didn't return his smile. The girl stood in the living room and folded her arms. Her lips, which Quinn found even more appealing without lipstick, pouted.

"*You* are responsible for situation?"

"I'm responsible for your safety tonight."

"What gives you the—"

"Excuse me, Miss Kosenko." Quinn walked right past the surprised girl, across the living room, and to the picture window. The bulletproof glass was cold to his touch. As he had hoped, it was tinted, like the windows of a limousine, so no one from the outside could see in.

He turned and faced her, moving into the center of the living room. With any operation, even glorified babysitting, the first rule was to stake your ground. "Sorry to interrupt. I needed to inspect the window."

She looked back in stony silence.

"I'm afraid I also need to check your bedroom and bath. It'll just take a second. May I?"

With a dismissive "what's next" raise of her eyebrows, she motioned with her hand for him to enter.

He felt her eyes follow him as he walked into the bedroom, which was decorated all in white. A white canopy topped the empty four-poster bed made of white-painted wood. A glass-covered fireplace, also framed in white wood, was unlit. The master bath, done in white marble, had no windows.

A glance at the coffered ceiling confirmed that, as with the other rooms, it had no crawl-space entry, and the vents on the walls were far too small for anyone to climb through. The suite shared no doors to any adjoining suites. The only way in or out was the door to the hallway.

When he walked back into the living room, Quinn caught her giving him an appraising look. As they made eye contact, her expression returned to its sulk.

Time for another peace offering. He took a step toward her, extending his hand. "I should've introduced myself. My name is—"

"I know your name, Mr. Quinn. Officer Doyle was kind

enough to inform me." The girl ignored his offered hand. Her tense body language told him to come no closer.

She'd pronounced "Mister" as "*mees*-tehr." Her speech was crisp and clear, and her Russian accent faint. Probably from her years living in London. But traces of her homeland still rang through.

He put his hand down, contemplating his next move.

The girl unfolded her arms and put her hands on her hips, tilting her head back. "What nonsense is this?" She looked him up and down. "Police escort greets me at airport? Then follows me everywhere I go? They take away my phone. And now I cannot go out at all?"

Doyle hadn't been far off in his assessment. If Quinn couldn't find a way to pacify this diva, it would be a long night. How could he make her understand the danger was real? "There have been threats—"

"Shtop!" the girl snapped. "I know, I know! Crank phone calls. I get them always. It comes with territory when you are famous in performing arts." Her ice-blue eyes flashed. "I had stalker in London. Did I give up my personal life? No! Courts put out warrant. Man was arrested. Simple."

It's not that simple this time, Quinn wanted to reply. *The Russian FSB is after you, not some obsessed fan.*

He forced himself to respond with bureaucrat-speak. "Miss Kosenko, it's standard policy to provide someone of your stature with adequate protection when—"

"Enough!" She raised one hand and pointed toward the foyer. "Already there are two policemen outside door. Now I must put up with third man *inside* my hotel suite?"

"I'll camp out here in the living room and try to stay out of your way." He managed another polite smile.

Anna strode over to the hotel phone and picked up the receiver. "You will lose smile when I call hotel security, report dangerous intruder in room."

"Then be sure to ask for Mr. Hathaway. He's head of security for the hotel. He insisted on our presence as a condition for you being allowed to stay here. Otherwise, you'd be in protective custody, in one of NYPD's downtown jail cells."

"*Ah!*" She slammed the phone down and glared at Quinn. Her lips parted, and her breath came in short pants. Her chest heaved beneath the cotton bathrobe, which was coming loose.

What was it that made some attractive women *really* hot when they were angry?

Quinn searched for words to defuse the situation. "I sincerely regret any inconvenience, Miss Kosenko."

"And *I* regret that at eleven o'clock on Friday night, in one of world's most exciting cities, I am going to take sleeping pill and go to *bed*. Good night!"

She cinched her bathrobe tight. Without waiting for a reply, she turned around, walked back into the bedroom, and closed the door behind her.

Two hours later

A LIGHT SNOWFALL BEGAN A LITTLE AFTER MIDNIGHT, sprinkling flecks of white on the frozen gray slush. Traffic had thinned at the late hour, and through the picture window, the yellow headlights of the cars moved by at a somnambulant pace.

Quinn sat at the end of the sofa nearest the window, his coat off and his 9mm still in its shoulder holster. From his corner, he could see all of the living room, bar, foyer, entrance door, and part of the closed bedroom door. Anna had not emerged from the bedroom and was, judging by the total silence, fast asleep.

A long night stretched ahead.

A faint whining sound perked up his ears.

He scanned the room. Nothing. An insect?

No, something electrical. Someone using a hairdryer in the next room?

But this suite was virtually soundproof. And the noise sounded like it was behind him. Impossible, as he had his back to the window and wall.

The sound grew louder.

In one motion Quinn stood and whirled around, his 9mm drawn and ready.

A drone hovered outside, like a helicopter, in the center of the picture window. It was painted black, but the bright city lights illuminated it as if it were on display.

Perhaps two feet wide, the small drone had an X-shaped frame with four propellers spinning at the ends of the four arms and another propeller atop its oval midsection. A small circle at the front glinted. The camera lens.

Quinn stepped away from the window, his mind churning. The drone was obviously there to spy. Anything else? No markings, no visible weaponry. But the midsection was bulky enough to hold a bomb. He couldn't take the chance.

Backing farther away, he holstered his gun back and took out his cell phone.

He tapped an app icon, then entered an encryption code. He pointed the phone lens at the drone and watched the screen as a series of incomprehensible numbers scrolled by.

In seconds, the red circle at the bottom of the screen flashed. The app had located the radio frequency controlling the drone. He pressed the green circle next to the red one.

In unison, the five propellers stopped.

Quinn moved closer to the window. The disabled drone, buffeted by the winds, spiraled down and away from the hotel. By the time the drone landed in a patch of snow on the sidewalk on the other side of the street, Quinn had closed the app and was making a phone call.

"Probably the friggin' paparazzi," Doyle commented after listening to Quinn's explanation. "Just the same, I'll have the bomb squad truck there in five. And I'll send Russo out right now to keep away any looky-loos."

The weather and late hour kept the street free of pedestrians, but Quinn watched from above as Russo exited the hotel and shivered in the cold, keeping a respectful distance from the drone. The occasional car slowed as it passed Russo, but the street had emptied by the time the white armored truck pulled up.

Two men in helmeted protective suits climbed out of the truck. The back of the truck opened, and a ramp dropped down. A four-wheeled, black metal robot rolled down the ramp and toward the drone.

The robot used its claws to pick up the drone. It paused for a few seconds—x-raying?—then it turned around and rolled back up the ramp and into the truck. The doors closed, the men climbed back in, and the truck took off into the night.

The operation had run like clockwork. The drone would be taken to a safe location where it would be analyzed and, if necessary, detonated.

Quinn turned away from the window and selected a bottle of water from the bar's refrigerator. The tension of the incident had left him thirsty, and the chilled water revitalized his dry throat.

He couldn't tell the girl about the drone, of course. Another secret that he had to keep from her. For the first time, he felt a twinge of empathy for her frustration. None of this was her doing.

The intel on the threat from the FSB was circumstantial but plausible. Her father, a prominent Russian journalist, had been critical of the regime—enough to earn him a spot near the top of the regime's enemies list. He had also, as the Director had drily put it, been of discreet "help to the West."

Imprisoned four years ago on trumped-up tax evasion charges, the unrepentant journalist had wasted away behind bars until a few weeks ago, when he'd died of what the Russian state media termed a "degenerative disorder."

The reality, confirmed by the smuggled toxicology report now in the hands of the CIA, was that the man had been slowly poisoned to death. It was a fate that had, in recent years, also befallen other enemies of the state.

Even in death, however, it was important to the Kremlin narrative that this man still be vilified as a disloyal activist and not in any way be portrayed as a martyr. To reinforce this, the

Kremlin had plans for a show trial—a posthumous trial—on manufactured treason charges.

The FSB allegedly had orders to neutralize any close associates of the dead man before they announced the show trial. The girl was not just his only child; she was also his only living blood relative. And now she was halfway around the world from Russia, in the largest city of their rival country. What better place for the FSB to take her life?

Quinn looked out the window at the snowflakes shimmering in the city lights.

The twist in all this was that the girl herself knew nothing.

Anna Marina Kosenko had moved to London as a teenager and been raised by her mother. She hadn't seen her estranged father since she'd left Russia. Her mother had passed away two years earlier, and Anna believed her father had also died of illness. The girl was innocent and had nothing to do with any of this neo-Cold War chess play.

Quinn touched the grip of his 9mm as he gazed out the window at the tracks left by the armored bomb disposal truck.

Soft piano notes sounded behind him.

Still on edge from the drone incident, he whipped around, his gun drawn.

The girl sat at the piano, clad in her bathrobe.

"I could not sleep." Her voice was soft, and her eyes heavy-lidded. "I took another sleeping pill. Will take effect in few minutes. Playing music helps me relax."

"Rachmaninoff is a good way to unwind." Quinn slipped his gun into his shoulder holster. The girl hadn't noticed it. "That sonata you played at tonight's concert was superb. Is that one of his preludes now?"

"Yes, in E flat major. Such a pretty little melody. You know music?" Her eyes showed a glimmer of interest.

"Part of my misspent youth."

A smile played at the corners of her lips. "Was not complete waste of youth if you learned about the great Rachmaninoff."

"He had a rather colorful personal life himself. But that's a discussion for another day."

The girl looked at him as her fingers caressed the keys. "Something tells me there is more to you than you let on."

"Perhaps the same can be said of you."

"Perhaps." In her drowsy state, the word came out as "porheps."

"And perhaps we should continue this discussion tomorrow, Miss Kosenko. It's late, and you're tired, and you have another concert to perform."

"Yes." The girl stood up. She blinked and ran a hand through her tousled hair. "I can feel sleeping pill now. If I stay, I might say something silly. But was good to talk. Now I find you interesting. Good night, Mr. Quinn."

Barefoot on the thick carpet, the girl padded back to her bedroom and closed the door.

Quinn breathed a sigh of relief at having finally broken the ice. He walked around the living room as he finished his bottle of water.

It was quite possible that on this assignment, nothing more would happen. There could be no attack at all. With the constant presence of the blue-uniformed New York police officers, any potential operations may have been called off.

He put the thought out of his mind. To be at peak alertness, he had to assume that the operation was on. The New York police were the front lines. They would escort the girl everywhere she went while in New York and would repel any initial assault.

But the attackers would surely have a plan B, a backup plan.

And Quinn's assignment was to stop *that*.

Saturday evening
Kronberg Concert Hall
New York City, New York

A COLD SNAP DROPPED THE TEMPERATURE INTO THE single digits, driving away the tourists and locals that normally filled the streets, forcing even the itinerant street vendors to seek the warmth of indoors. The few bold pedestrians that ventured into the frigid air hunched their shoulders and exhaled little dragon-puffs of white fog.

In contrast, the crowd entering Kronberg Hall seemed oblivious to the chill and was even merrier than the group the night before. Happy chatter and greetings floated through the night as Quinn picked his way among topcoats and hats and furs, scanning the faces of the concertgoers.

The concert hall was a century-old red brick-and-limestone structure situated on a corner in the Theater District. After examining the throng at the entrance, Quinn retraced his steps from the previous evening and walked all the way around the building.

He'd received the results of the drone analysis via a text message late that morning. The drone held a camera, nothing more. Some kind of technology that could see through the window tinting. Most likely, the text had stated, it was all the effort of some enterprising paparazzi, hoping to get a photograph of the young woman at an indiscrete moment.

That incident was over. But it was no reason to let down his guard.

"The Kremlin is still angry about the Magnitsky Act," the CIA Director had warned at the briefing. "The situation with increased sanctions has raised tensions even higher. When they start this show trial, they want it to run smoothly, without any embarrassing interference from the West. By taking the girl out here, the Russians get two for one. They get rid of the girl, and, at the same time, they can blame her death on violent crime in America."

The Director's logic was impeccable. The drone had been a mere nuisance. The real threat was still out there.

The side street off Seventh Avenue was empty, save for a few cars making their way through the slush. Away from the well-lit, ornate Beaux-Arts facade of the building front, the side of the concert hall devolved into a wall of ugly brick punctuated by dark windows and empty fire escapes.

He slowed his step as he turned into the back alley and saw a truck backed up to the loading dock. Two men were unloading boxes from the back of the truck.

"Doyle," Quinn spoke into his earpiece microphone. "The loading dock. Truck. Two men."

The raspy voice responded, "Does the truck say Empire Distributors? Both men in uniform, one bald, one short hair?"

"Yes."

"They're clean. They deliver the booze once a week. All deliveries have to be cleared in advance, and we ran background checks on both men." Doyle added, "Hey, your princess in the dressing room here seems to be a little nicer than she was last night. You musta softened her up."

"I think she, like us, will be happy when this is over."

"You got that right." He chuckled and clicked off.

Quinn turned into the narrow side alley.

Up ahead, a hand-holding couple rounded the corner and walked toward him. After a few yards and seeing that the alley held nothing of interest, they stopped and went back.

He followed the couple onto Seventh Avenue and into the main entrance of the concert hall.

In the lobby, the chattering crowd, in their tuxedos and gowns and jewelry, looked like a clone of the group from the previous evening. When the chimes rang, signaling the concertgoers to take their seats, Quinn was already back in his sniper's nest, double-checking his riflescope calibration for the short distances inside the concert hall.

The concert was, as expected, the same program as the previous evening. Yet Anna Marina Kosenko brought the same intensity as she had before, treating each piece as if playing it for the first time.

The change came with the encore. Instead of the showy, flashy piece of the previous evening, she chose something subdued. And familiar. The charming prelude that the sleepy-eyed girl had played in her bathrobe late last night.

He shut the music out of his mind and looked through the

scope, surveying the stage. Nothing. Switching to his binoculars, he swept back and forth across the audience.

Both nights Quinn had noted the same demographic distribution. The high-end seats of the front rows and the terraced box seats held older, affluent attendees, and the twenty-something music students again sat in the cheap seats in the back. His binoculars lingered on the elderly-looking couples in the spacious box seats and then on the middle-aged patrons in the front rows.

She was nearing the end of her encore.

He switched back to the scope and scanned the stage, then the front rows.

Something isn't right.

What was it? His scope swept the front rows again.

The well-dressed crowd sat politely, their hands in their laps or holding their programs. But terrorists and assassins were young men in their twenties and thirties. Most of this crowd was well over fifty, and at least half of them were women.

There.

Near the far side of the front row, a plump, fiftyish woman was applying lipstick. That was what had bothered him. Rude, but unremarkable. His scope moved on along the row of rapt, upturned faces.

On the other side of the curving front row, the scope picked up another woman, younger than the first, also applying lipstick. He stopped and focused on this woman.

A coincidence? Maybe they weren't interested in the music, but concerned about how they looked as they left the concert hall. Perhaps their husbands enjoyed classical music, and these women went along for the social activity.

His scope panned to the end of the row, then began its slow sweep back.

The skin on the back of Quinn's neck crawled when a third woman, this time in the center of the front row, also began applying lipstick.

Three women in the front row, all applying lipstick at the same time.

Perhaps it was nothing. But his gut told him otherwise. Everyone in the front rows paid close attention to the music. Brows furrowed. Lips pursed.

These three women remained stone-faced.

With a lingering arpeggio, the encore ended.

The hall went quiet as the last notes faded away. A pause, then the concert hall erupted as the audience stood and cheered and applauded with all the gusto of the previous evening's crowd.

Yet the applause, echoing off the high ceilings, sounded sinister.

Quinn's heartbeat quickened. He dialed back his scope so he could see all three women at the same time. What the hell was going on with these women and their damned lipstick? They were standing, as was everyone else in the front rows, holding long-stemmed red roses to throw onto the stage.

Anna Marina Kosenko, a gracious smile on her face, made her way forward from the piano and stood among the first-tossed red roses already strewn on the stage. More roses landed at her feet.

Quinn focused his scope on the hands of the three women

and noticed the gold metal lipstick holders clutched in their hands along with their red roses. The women drew back their arms to toss the roses, still clutching their lipstick holders.

The three red roses, along with countless others, flew toward the stage. As the roses arced through the air, the scope picked up flashes of gold glinting in the floodlights.

A quick glance back confirmed what Quinn already knew. The three women now stood, empty-handed, clapping.

"Doyle! Russo! Something's up." Quinn spoke into his microphone. "The stage. Get—"

Before he could finish his sentence, a sharp *bang* came from the far side of the stage. A cloud of white smoke, several feet wide, spread across the stage.

"Cover the girl!" shouted Quinn.

Through the smoke at the far end of the stage, Doyle bolted out like a tackle charging a quarterback. In one motion, he leaped forward, arms outstretched, and grabbed the girl around the waist. She shrieked as she fell to the stage, with Doyle's bearlike body on top of her.

From the other side of the stage, Russo had run out at the same time as Doyle. He dropped to one knee on top of Doyle, his knee on the small of the policeman's back. Russo drew his gun and peered out toward the audience, trying to see past the floodlights.

A second *bang* came from the other side of the stage, and another cloud of white smoke spread out from that side toward the center.

At the sound, Russo, still kneeling on top of Doyle, went into a two-handed shooting stance and pivoted to the side, pointing his gun toward the cloud of white smoke. He scanned back and forth, searching for an attacker, but none appeared, just smoke.

Through the scope, Quinn saw Russo's lips moving, cursing in frustration.

Screams came from the audience at the explosions. Now a rumble swelled from the stunned crowd. In the back rows, people began heading for the exits.

Quinn scanned the stage and front rows. No one rushed the stage from the front or the sides. His scope picked up a glint of gold from the middle of the stage.

The third lipstick holder.

No smoke, no bang had come from that one. Perhaps it was delayed. Or a dud. Or—

"Get the girl off the stage!" Quinn ordered.

Russo stood, staggering as he took a step back. Doyle pushed himself up on one arm, then the other. He'd taken a hard fall, but with one arm, he grabbed the girl around her waist and got to one knee, then paused.

Why were they moving so freaking slow?

"Everyone get the hell off the stage!" Quinn yelled into his microphone. "Now, dammit!"

Doyle had gotten the girl to her knees. Russo lifted her up by her right arm. Everything on the stage seemed to be happening lethargically.

Quinn pulled away from the scope and, with his naked eye, scanned the concert hall.

Backup. No one rushed the stage. The audience members on the main floor chattered to one another in worried voices, looking around as if waiting to be told what to do.

His eyes went to the box seats in the terraces. The older

couples still occupied their seats, some standing, some still sitting, all watching.

Except for one.

The middle box seat in the top terrace, a box almost as high up as Quinn's position and with a commanding view of the stage, was empty.

An elderly couple had been sitting there. Quinn remembered them. They had moved with care when they had come in and taken their seats. The old man had used a cane. It would've been an effort for them to get up and get out that fast.

He adjusted the scope and zoomed in on the box until he could see every fold in the thick velvet curtains behind the seats. No one there. The old couple had gotten up and left—that was all.

Sudden movement caught Quinn's eye. The folds of the thick velvet curtain in the empty box seat stirred.

Keeping an eye on the curtain, Quinn glanced back at the stage. The girl stood, supporting herself with one arm around Doyle's shoulders and one arm around Russo's shoulders. Her head hung down as if she were sleepy. Russo stepped away from her and to his right, trying to lead them off the stage, brandishing his gun toward the audience in a sweeping half-circle.

In the darkness behind the seats in the empty box, Quinn's scope picked up a black rifle barrel emerging from behind the velvet curtain.

Backup had waited until the target was in clear view.

His heart pounding like a hammer against his chest,

Quinn focused the crosshairs on the curtain behind and up from the rifle barrel, then he pulled the trigger.

A *crack* resounded in the hall. The thick curtains moved as the barrel jerked up, and the rifle flew forward. A black-clad figure lurched from behind the curtains into the box seats, grabbing for the falling rifle.

The gunman was wounded but very much alive.

Quinn focused the crosshairs on the shooter's head and tracked the moving target.

Now.

He pulled the trigger.

Another *crack* echoed across the high ceiling. The scope picked up a flash of dark mist as the top of the shooter's head exploded. Fragments of bone and tissue splattered onto the empty seats, and drops of blood glistened bright red in the illuminated reticle. Screams came from the boxes on either side.

The black-clad figure crumpled in a heap to the floor of the box seat.

Three hours later
The Grand Empire Hotel

"YOUR HUNCH WAS RIGHT, MICHAEL," WILL, QUINN'S field supervisor, spoke in his earpiece. "It was gas. Odorless, colorless gas, but dangerously toxic all the same."

"I thought so when I saw Anna and both policemen staggering, trying to get up."

Quinn strode through the hotel lobby, glancing around to make sure he was alone. Two bored-looking desk clerks focused on their cell phones, and the lounge had a sprinkling of couples absorbed in quiet conversation. No one looked up as he walked by.

He fixed a nondescript smile on his face, trying to blend in as just another hotel guest arriving back from a late evening out. Inside, he was still a jangle of nerves, his mind full of questions as he reviewed everything that had happened again and again.

He spoke *sotto voce* into his microphone as he walked across the marble floor toward the elevator. "What else do we know, Will?"

"It looks like the gas was a highly potent version of something called carfentanil. Remember the Moscow theater hostage crisis? Similar to what the Russians used then, but updated and much stronger. Here, it was delivered as an aerosol from that middle lipstick holder. In a few seconds, you're sleepy. In a few minutes, you never wake up. Fortunately, the paramedics were all over them, and the ambulance got them to the hospital in no time."

"So, the lipstick holders on either side were smoke grenades, designed to be a distraction while the gas took care of the target."

"Yes. Plus, of course, the shooter as backup."

"Clever bastards."

"As always." Will paused. "The shooter was DOA, of course. We'll have more info on him by the morning. The 'lipstick ladies' and the old couple in the box seat vanished in the chaos. The surveillance cameras might turn up something."

"The policemen, they're okay?"

"Yeah. Doyle and Russo are both being debriefed. Doyle, by the way, says he wants to buy you a beer the next time you're in town."

"Tell him it's a deal." Quinn walked into the empty, glass-walled elevator and pushed the button for the penthouse floor. "How's the girl?"

"She was pretty shaken up, but she's safely back in her hotel suite. I imagine she'll be a bit more cooperative tonight. The two NYPD officers on the night shift are guarding her door and are expecting you. And the Director asked me to pass on his congratulations for keeping the girl safe. A rough night for concertgoers, but things could have gone much worse."

"Thanks, Will."

The elevator door closed, and Quinn leaned against the back wall, half-closing his eyes. The subsiding adrenaline left him tired and drained. Ugly scenes from the concert hall kept replaying in his mind. The whole thing had been too damn close. A couple of seconds the other way and things could indeed have gone much worse.

The elevator took him up through the soaring atrium, quiet floor after quiet floor. At the penthouse entrance, the two policemen on guard nodded to him as they opened the door to the suite.

The scene that greeted Quinn as he walked in pushed aside the dark images of the concert hall. It looked like some sort of painting—perhaps a nineteenth-century portrait.

The girl sat at the piano in the living room, playing something peaceful. Atop the piano, a half-full glass of red wine sat next to a crystal vase full of red roses. Framing her, in the world outside the picture window, the steady snowfall covered the city of New York in elegant layers of pure white.

The hotel suite was no longer the hostile territory it had seemed at the beginning of the previous evening. Now it was a welcoming sanctuary, and the music nourished Quinn's hungry soul. His spirits lifted as he walked into the living room and put his suitcase down next to the piano.

Without looking up from the keys, the girl spoke as if talking to herself. "All I have ever wanted is to live my life and play my music. I have never harmed one soul."

Quinn hesitated, not sure what to say.

"Tell me, Mr. Quinn." She rested her hands on the keys. Her eyes misted as she looked at him. "Who would want to harm me?"

She was the same girl as last night, but it seemed like a different person was speaking. Harsh reality had intruded on her life. Gone was the dismissive diva. Gone, as well, was part of her innocence.

He started to reply and stopped himself. It was all too complex. It wasn't the right time or place, and it went beyond his purview anyway. What to say? "The man who was after you tonight won't bother you again."

She seemed embarrassed. "Last night, when I go to bed, I was angry. Then I think to myself, perhaps I get consolation prize. If I must have guard in my hotel room, at least he is tall and *krasivyy*—handsome—and he has kind eyes."

"I'm glad your opinion of me has improved."

"Later, when I come back out and play piano, I find out also that you like music and are *kulturny.*"

"Not all of us policemen are philistines."

"Now, tonight, you save my life." She looked at him with curiosity. "You are some sort of soldier?"

"Used to be."

"You are not just policeman. What are you really?"

"I'm responsible for your safety the rest of the night, Miss Kosenko, until the police escort comes in the morning to take you to the airport. I'm afraid we'll have to leave it at that."

The girl reached for her glass of wine. "Must we be formal? Call me Anna. I can call you Michael?"

"Of course, Anna."

She stood and walked over to the suite's small bar. Another glass of red wine sat atop the granite counter. She caressed the stem of the glass with her free hand. "They say there is lesson in everything, Michael. I think I have learned something tonight, something I never knew before."

"And what is that?"

"That there is more." She paused. "I cannot believe I say these words—that there is more to life than my music. That life, it is to be lived in full. Each day."

"I suppose so."

"You've probably never had Russian wine." She picked up the glass. "This is good cabernet. From coastal regions along Black Sea. I bring it with me when I go on tour." She walked around the bar and handed it to him. "It is least I can do to say thank you."

When he'd entered the living room, Quinn had thought she was still wearing her black evening gown. Now, as she stepped close, he realized that she'd changed into a black negligee, of a fabric so thin it was almost translucent. In the soft glow of the recessed ceiling lights, tantalizing glimpses of fair skin showed through here and there.

As she placed the glass of wine in his hand, she took another step closer. The clinging nightgown delineated every curve of her figure. Her blue eyes looked up at him, and her blonde hair, a bit tousled, fell just so over each breast. Quinn inhaled scents of orchid and jasmine.

She's irresistible, dammit, and she knows it. Quinn took a step back. He placed the glass of wine back on the granite counter.

"We're crossing some boundaries here, Anna. You know I can't drink on duty. And since you're dressed nicely for bed, it's probably a good idea that you go to bed. I'll set up camp on the living room sofa. Is there anything else you need?"

Her lips formed into a pout. "There is one thing. Come with me."

She strode across the living room, toward the bedroom. As she passed the piano, her right hand picked up all of the long-stemmed roses from the vase atop the piano. The stems dripped a trail of water drops onto the beige carpet as she carried the roses into the bedroom.

Quinn followed, mystified.

Inside the cozy bedroom, the fireplace was lit, and an assortment of candles flickered on the wood mantel, casting soft shadows on the walls surrounding the four-poster, canopied bed. The pearl-white duvet was turned down.

Quinn stopped just past the front door. What a setup. He could feel the warmth from the fireplace. His own senses, still tasting the orchid and jasmine, stirred. He looked at the girl standing a few feet to his side and put polite authority into his voice.

"And just what is it you wanted me to see in here?"

Anna stepped toward him and held up the handful of roses. She squeezed the stems, her knuckles turning white and her fingers wriggling with the concentrated effort. Then, with an exaggerated, sweeping motion of her arm, she opened her fingers and scattered the roses onto the bed.

She stepped closer to him until their bodies almost touched. Spreading wide the fingers of her right hand, she held her palm up close so Quinn could see the dots of blood where the thorns had pricked her skin.

Trickles of dark red blood oozed down her fingers and palm.

"You are responsible for my safety tonight?" Her blue eyes searched his.

"Yes, but—"

Standing on her tiptoes, she leaned forward so that her body brushed against him. Her breasts swelled against the flimsy fabric of the plunging neckline.

"Then you must climb onto bed with me and help me safely gather up roses. Do you want me back at hospital tonight, cut and bleeding from something that happened right here in hotel room?"

"Anna—"

She put a blood-tinged finger to his lips as she brought her mouth up to his.

"*Do you?*"

THE GODDESS OF THE DEEP

A MICHAEL QUINN SHORT STORY

KEVIN SCOTT OLSON

She is a woman, therefore may be woo'd
She is a woman, therefore may be won.

— SHAKESPEARE

THE GODDESS OF THE DEEP

Naval Amphibious Base
Coronado, California

"I THINK WE CAN DO BETTER, SIR," SAID PETTY OFFICER
Hansen. "Shall we try again?"

Michael Quinn gave a thumbs-up as he treaded water.
Hansen, kicking in place a few feet away, gave the go-ahead
nod. Quinn pressed the valve on his BCD, his inflatable
diving vest, and slowly sank below the surface of the sea.

The blue sky and white clouds disappeared from view. The
gray liquid world of the Pacific Ocean took over, darkening as
he descended.

As his fins gently touched the sandy bottom, the twin
eighty-pound tanks on his back felt weightless. He kicked up a
few feet and adjusted his BCD until he achieved neutral
buoyancy.

This was his last day of training, and so far, things had

gone well. He had reacquainted himself with every piece of gear he might need—the Draeger rebreather, his dive knife, the updated console with its gauges and dive computer. And an exhilarating, adrenaline edge accompanied combat dive training.

Even if he had to put up with what was about to happen next.

He kicked in place and waited.

Something slammed his head and neck forward. His facemask was ripped off. Then his mouthpiece.

Quinn reached out to grab his facemask before it floated away in the current. With his other hand, he retrieved his mouthpiece and put it back in his mouth. He exhaled.

But when he inhaled, he almost choked. No air.

He groped behind his back and found the air intake line. It floated freely in the water, unhooked.

Quinn cursed. He pulled the line around in front of him. Not only was it unhooked—the air intake line was tied in a knot.

His mind sent calming messages to the primeval panic rising in his gut. *Relax. You can handle this.*

He pulled the air intake line close to his eyes. No time to put the facemask, which still dangled from his wrist, back on. His eyes stung, and his vision blurred from the cold saltwater, but he could see well enough to fix the air line.

The knot refused to budge. His lungs burned, and he felt an enormous pressure on his chest. He fought the instinctive urge to shoot for the surface. Ignoring the wave of dizziness that marked the onset of oxygen deprivation, he focused on his thumb and index finger pulling at the knot loop.

Precious seconds later, the knot loosened then finally gave. He untied the knot and slipped his fingers down to the end of the line.

His fingers reached around in back and found the tank, then the valve. Then came the reassuring *click* as the air intake line fitted back in place. He took a deep breath through his mouthpiece and kicked his way up.

When his head broke the surface, Quinn removed his mouthpiece and breathed in gulps of sea air. He rubbed his eyes, and when he opened them, he found Petty Officer Hansen floating a few feet away, treading water.

"Well done, sir. Improved by five seconds, even with the knot." Hansen looked at his watch. "I believe you're ready. Let's swim back to shore and take one of the IBS boats out. We need to make sure you can do this in rough water."

Although they were both SEALs, Hansen addressed Quinn as "sir." This deference came in part from Quinn's superior rank as a Lieutenant Commander and in part from rumors about Quinn's missions. A few details had invariably leaked back to the base.

As they swam along the surface, Quinn noted how quickly the days had passed. The call had come only five days ago: Go to Coronado and train for a mission that would involve a serious amount of time in the water.

Quinn received no other details except that he'd be diving in a hostile environment. As with many covert missions, the protocol was hurry up, get ready, then stand by.

He turned his head to the left. At the far end of the beach, in the pounding surf near an outcrop of large black rocks, a group of SEALs practiced amphibious entries and landings with the small IBS boats. As the SEALs made it over the waves, their exuberant yells sounded over the roar of the surf.

Quinn kicked on. Had it really been five years since he'd left the SEALs?

He cleared away a piece of kelp from his mask. The water was turning frothy. They'd almost reached the beach.

Quinn and Petty Officer Tommy Hansen had become fast friends during training. Hansen was in his early twenties and had been a SEAL for three years. A soft-spoken Midwesterner, he had short, reddish-brown hair and freckled skin. His upbringing showed in his work ethic and respectful manners.

They walked out of the shallows onto the sand and untethered the IBS boat waiting for them. The late afternoon sun cast golden light onto the beach as they launched into the gunmetal sea.

Hansen took the boat out past the surf, then steered it to a windy area with rough, choppy water. He ran Quinn through a final gauntlet of diving drills designed to simulate the adverse conditions of either an attacker, rough seas, or, in a worst-case scenario, both.

The common enemy of divers is entanglement, and Quinn was put to the test.

He found himself repeatedly snared in hook-laden fishing line, sometimes with his air intake line unhooked, while the restless sea tossed him around. Other drills had him tangled every which way in thick rope tied to an anchor, forcing him to use his knife to cut himself free without his facemask and mouthpiece.

His muscles ached and his lungs burned, but he put

himself into his one-step-at-a-time zone and worked through each drill.

By the time they dragged the boat back onto the beach, the sun had disappeared below the horizon. The evening's first stars shone in the sky, and the sea turned as dark as coal.

Except for the tides. Hansen pointed out to sea. "Check 'em out, sir."

Every once in a while, some sort of algae traveled to the Pacific and, for a brief time, made moving water bioluminescent. Now, as the waves crashed and the tide rolled in, the froth glowed a beautiful blue, bright enough to seem otherworldly.

The blue tide was considered good luck. Quinn took it as an omen of success for his next mission, whatever it was to be.

Hansen sat on the edge of the boat as he removed his fins. "Sir, if you're up for a little R&R this evening, I was wondering if you'd like to go for a beer at the cave. Your reputation preceded your coming here, and it'd be an honor to buy you a cold one."

Quinn looked out at the blue tide. He was exhausted, but he was also hungry and thirsty.

"The honor is mine, Officer Hansen, as long as you let me buy the beer."

Three hours later
The Mermaid Lounge
San Diego, California

TOPPED WITH GRILLED ONIONS, JUICY BEEFSTEAK tomatoes, and melted Monterey Jack cheese, the charbroiled beef burger in Quinn's hands ranked among the best he had ever tasted.

He followed his last bite with a swig from his bottle of cold Negra Modelo, then he leaned his chair back against the cool wall of the cave. Next to him, Hansen also leaned against the wall, his hand loosely curled around his bottle of beer. The remains of his burger lay on the paper plate in front of him.

The Mermaid Lounge, a longtime popular hangout for SEALs, was rarely called by its real name. To its patrons, it felt like a cave and looked like a cave and thus had always been known as "the cave."

Quinn sipped his beer. The place had no windows, low ceilings, and dim lighting so subdued that the humble place may as well have been lit with a few candles. The waitresses used little flashlights to read the checks.

Men in T-shirts and dog tags crowded the small tables, a few with girlfriends in tow, most in groups looking for girls. Quinn picked out pieces of conversation amid the shouts and laughter. Many of the men were either back from a mission or were training for one.

Man's desire to enjoy food and drink while letting off steam had its roots far back in history, probably to when men sought shelter in a *real* cave. The only difference was that instead of gathering around a fire to celebrate, the men now gathered around a circular stage and a shiny brass pole.

He looked around the room. Behind the bar was the faded mural of Poseidon riding his sea chariot over the waves, one arm poised to throw his trident. Old nautical memorabilia decorated the opposite wall—an anchor, a harpoon, a vintage spear gun—interspersed with color photographs of the club dancers.

"From the poster, I take it we're going to see a 'lovely lady' tonight, Hansen?"

"A very special one, sir. I know you're tired. Hope you don't mind."

"Not at all. The fairer sex is one of my favorite pursuits."

"If you don't mind my asking, sir, do you have a girlfriend?"

"Not at present. With me, relationships with the opposite sex are a bit like diving. They can be enjoyable, even thrilling. But you want to avoid entanglements."

Hansen grinned. "Forever, sir?"

"Maybe." Quinn looked down at his Modelo. "I certainly enjoy female companionship. One of life's greatest treasures. But I won't settle. It would have to be just the right girl.

"It takes time to really know someone. And you need to be there for them. The demands of what I do make that challenging. Impossible, really. So, for the foreseeable future, my mission is to sail my ship alone."

"Forever is a long time, sir. How about another beer?"

Quinn looked up and nodded.

Hansen ordered another round from the short-skirted waitress.

As the waitress walked away, the lights darkened in front of the round stage, and the club announcer walked up to the microphone and tapped it. The club speakers crackled, and the slick-haired announcer tapped the microphone. The jukebox, which had been playing country music, fell silent.

Their waitress appeared and placed the two beers on the small table. She took a good look at Quinn, sprawled on the tilted chair. Then she leaned over, displayed a generous portion of her bosom, and asked if there was anything more she could do for him.

He shook his head, and she turned away and disappeared into the darkness.

A lone spotlight fell on the announcer at the microphone.

"*Gentlemen!* And ladies, too, of course." The announcer's words came out in a smooth baritone. "Welcome, all of you, to this evening at the Mermaid Lounge."

The crowd buzzed with modest enthusiasm.

"We are pleased to present to you this evening's *star* attraction."

The speakers played a prerecorded drumroll at a low volume, and the room fell silent.

The announcer grabbed the microphone stand, tilted it toward himself, then gestured broadly, turning like a ringmaster to face all sides of the crowded room.

"My shipmates!" His sonorous voice drew out his words in dramatic fashion. "When you're out on those savage and solitary seas, do you crave the company of a *lovely lady?*"

A couple of claps came from the back of the crowd.

"When your ship is thousands of miles from home, when you go out on deck and gaze up at the moon and stars, do you long for the warmth of a fine, *fine woman?*"

The crowd delivered more applause and shouts of "Hell

yeah!" and "Damn straight!" The volume of the drum roll rose a notch.

"We have for you tonight, my friends, *pleasures* untold, *treasures* untold, from a *sultry,* shipshape lass, one guaranteed to touch the heart of *every* sailor here!"

The shouts from the crowd blended into a low rumble. The drumroll increased another notch.

"Yes, my shipmates, we have for you a sweetheart who will keep you *warm* those cold, cold nights at sea!"

More claps. Someone shouted, "I'll take her!"

"A young maiden who will be your safe port in *any* storm!"

The drumroll grew louder.

"Bring her on!" someone called from the back of the room.

"A lady whose charms you will never, *ever* forget, my good lads!" The announcer breathed into the microphone. "Ah yes, my friends. You'll like the cut of her jib, you'll savor every inch of this fine lady, from her *gorgeous* stem to her *exquisite* stern!"

Men banged their beer bottles on the tables. The drum roll reverberated off the walls of the cave as boisterous shouts filled the room.

"My friends," the announcer raised his voice, "we bring to you tonight the Lady of the Lake! The Temptress of the Tides! The Siren of the Seven Seas!"

Quinn cupped his hand to be heard over the noise and turned to Hansen. "This is quite an introduction."

"She's worth it, sir," he called back.

The announcer tilted the microphone closer and shouted over the booming drumroll. "My shipmates, feast your eyes on … the one, the only … Misty Fathom, *the Goddess of the Deep!*"

Rock music thundered from the speakers as the announcer scurried away. The crowd whistled and cheered as red and green and blue lights circled the edge of the stage.

A curvaceous, feminine figure, still shrouded in shadow, walked forward and placed her hand on the brass pole.

The lights moved to the center of the stage, illuminating her.

The crowd roared.

Misty Fathom, the Goddess of the Deep, was a fetching sea goddess indeed. Her eyes were a pretty teal-green, and her lips shone with turquoise lip gloss. Her skin was smooth and tanned, and specks of purple and silver glittered on her cheeks and forehead.

Her long hair hung down to her waist in rope-thick strands of blue and green and silver, the mane of a mermaid, crowned by a pearl-encrusted tiara. Long earrings of pearls with tiny pink shells dangled from her ears, matching the bracelets on her wrists and the multilayered necklace around her neck.

She wore a shimmering, low-cut dress made of thin fabric resembling the shiny scales of an exotic fish, in shades of purple and pearl and aquamarine. The dress hung on her bare shoulders by the thinnest of spaghetti straps and stopped at her upper thighs.

Below the dress, fishnet stockings stretched down her legs to pearl-colored platform shoes with crisscross straps and stiletto heels. In her right hand, she carried a silver trident encrusted with stones that glittered like milky-white diamonds.

The Goddess of the Deep gripped the brass pole with one

hand and circled around, waving her trident as the crowd shouted and whistled. Then she turned her back to the audience, stood with her legs apart, removed her tiara, and dropped it on the stage.

She shook her waist-long mane of multicolored hair side to side while she used the tines of her trident to slowly slide the spaghetti strap off each shoulder. Then she turned to face forward, posing with a leg forward and her hands on her hips, her dress on the verge of falling off.

The crowd, already under her spell, whistled and whooped for more.

"Okay, she's hot," said Quinn.

The Goddess wrapped one leg around the pole, leaned back until her mane of hair almost touched the ground, and slowly spun around. As she did so, she unzipped her thin dress about halfway, letting the top half of the dress drop down to her waist, exposing her naked upper torso. Her firm breasts jutted upward.

A thunderous chorus of shouts and yells of appreciation arose from the crowd.

Now the Goddess spun the other way around the pole, this time unzipping her dress all the way. She pulled it off and dropped it on the floor, leaving her clad only in her shoes, stockings, and a turquoise bikini bottom.

The cave reverberated with whoops and hollers, and the walls vibrated as the men banged their beer bottles on the tables.

The Goddess danced to the blaring rock music. She shimmied her shoulders, rolled her hips, and blew kisses to the crowd. She strutted around the perimeter of the stage, holding her silver trident over the heads of the men seated closest to her as if she were a queen knighting them.

Her blue-green mane of mermaid hair tossed and swayed, and her voluptuous body twisted and turned to the pounding beat. Rivulets of sweat dripped down her supple skin, sending glistening beads of perspiration flying off into the mesmerized crowd.

Quinn leaned his head against the wall of the cave. With the beer and good food in his belly, his tired body felt content.

He noticed Hansen also leaning his head against the wall, close enough to Quinn to speak without shouting.

"She's a beauty, all right," remarked Quinn.

"She is, and I'm going to marry her." Hansen's eyes remained focused on the Goddess.

"Yeah, right. A strip—" Quinn was about to laugh, then he stopped himself. "Seriously?"

"Yes, sir. We're engaged."

"Okay, then." Quinn raised his eyebrows. "So, you've been going out with her for awhile, then?"

"A month."

"A month." Quinn put his beer bottle on the table.

"It's like this, sir." Hansen gripped his bottle of beer. "I saw her for the first time when I came here for a night out with the guys. We went out for a drink after her shift ended. And, well, sometimes you just know. And I knew, that first night, that this was the girl for me.

"Sometimes these things just happen. I read somewhere that a King of England abdicated his throne to get his woman. When you've found your soulmate, you just know. And you do what it takes to make it work.

"We've been together ever since we met. Her real name is Rachel. She's a student at Mesa College. The dancing isn't forever; it's to pay her bills. She wants to be a dental assistant. More important to me, she wants to be my wife. I proposed last week, and she said yes. That's all I need to know."

"All you need to know? For marriage? For God's sake, Hansen. Look, I know she's gorgeous, but—"

"But what, sir?"

The pulsating music swelled to a crescendo. The Goddess held both her arms in the air, her body undulating to the music, her long mermaid mane swaying to and fro.

"A hundred different things, Hansen. She looks like she might be a bit of a wild child, to put it mildly. There might be a rough character or two in her life."

"You're quite right, sir." Hansen nodded. "She's made some poor choices in the past. There are some issues. I'm aware of all that, and I can handle it. But she has a good heart. With that going for us, there's nothing that can't be worked out."

"You seem pretty confident."

"I am, sir. I believe you can handle any mission in life if you have the will."

"Well, yes," Quinn admitted. "I suppose you can."

The music blasted out its climax. The Goddess of the Deep posed on the stage like a Greek statue, legs apart, shoulders proudly thrust back, her beautiful body gleaming with sweat. She tilted her face up, closed her eyes, and hoisted the trident high.

"And she is my mission," finished Hansen.

"I see." Quinn looked up at the girl, then over at Hansen. *So be it.* He raised his bottle of beer in salute. "Well, Hansen,

165

it's not every day a man finds a goddess. Good luck to you on your mission."

"Thank you." Hansen turned toward Quinn. He raised his bottle of beer in respectful salute. "And good luck to you on yours, sir."

NIGHT DIVE

A MICHAEL QUINN SHORT STORY

KEVIN SCOTT OLSON

No man was ever alone on the sea.

— ERNEST HEMINGWAY

NIGHT DIVE

Late evening
Agua Rica Bay, the Caribbean

A NIGHT SCUBA DIVE, DONE FOR PLEASURE, CAN BE A journey into another universe. Marine life of fantastic shapes and colors, from gossamer jellyfish to glowing squid, emerge from their hiding places to feed and to court. If the dive is blessed by a full moon, the diver can douse his torch and watch the sea creatures shimmer under the stars while the ocean itself glows with streaks of bioluminescence.

Michael Quinn, perched on the edge of the rubber Zodiac boat, held his facemask in his hands and looked around while he adjusted the strap. There would be no such sightseeing tonight.

Blanketed by clouds, the sky was a moonless, starless void that melded into a Caribbean as black as coal. Just as well. This dive was all business.

He slipped his facemask on and glanced to his left.

O'Donnell, his coxswain for this mission, waited at the other end, a silhouette against the sky. Neither man spoke. The only sound was the lapping of the waves.

The silhouette nodded once. Quinn slid off the boat and into the sea.

Instantly, the liquid world surrounded him in its darkness. Now the only sound was his breathing, its slow rhythm magnified by the regulator. A curious calmness set in—a tranquility born of the silence and loss of gravity that began each dive mission. He kicked up, gave O'Donnell the okay sign, and sank below the surface.

At twenty feet, he adjusted his dive vest until he achieved neutral buoyancy. Although he'd checked his gear on the boat, he felt for it again. His dive computer and compass were strapped to his wrist. Strapped to one side of his belt was his black MK3 combat dive knife, a treasure from his SEAL days. On the other side, his fingers gripped a new addition: his HK P11 underwater pistol.

A 7.62mm weapon, the HK P11 fired five bullets that were actually stiletto-pointed darts, effective underwater up to thirty feet. After two hours of training with the HK, he'd adapted to the oddly short barrel and chose it—rather than a spear gun—because it could be holstered and left his hands free. Most important, should he encounter hostiles underwater, it gave him multiple bullets.

He tilted forward and began a rhythmic kick-and-breathe. He rounded the rocky promontory hiding the Zodiac, checked his compass, and made a straight line toward the coastline of Agua Rica Bay. Kicking with the long dive fins always seemed effortless in waters this calm.

In theory, this mission was clear: Locate a pair of JL-2 Giant Wave missiles hidden in an underwater silo, about a quarter-mile away.

Those missiles weren't supposed to be there. They weren't supposed to be anywhere in the Western hemisphere.

Generalissimo Rafael Guzman Calderon, the dictator who ran the People's Republic of Agua Rica with an iron fist, had purchased them from a cash-starved North Korea. The Giant Wave missiles were intercontinental-range SLBMs—submarine-launched ballistic missiles. Of Chinese origin, they were designed for deployment aboard the People's Liberation Army Type 094 submarine. Payload up to a 1,000-kiloton warhead.

The missiles—if they were there—had a range of over 4,000 miles. Thus, they threatened not only the neighboring Caribbean countries but also the United States.

Diplomatic efforts were going nowhere. Calderon vehemently denied possession of any weapons as powerful as missiles. Such accusations were nothing but Western propaganda, he said. Agua Rica was a peace-loving country that wished nothing more than to be left alone. And Calderon denied, for "security reasons," any and all requests to allow inspection of his country and the surrounding waters.

Calderon's army guarded Agua Rica Bay relentlessly, and they would fire upon any unauthorized vessel entering their waters without warning. Neighboring Caribbean countries, in high-level, off-the-record conversations, pleaded with the United States for assistance.

If Quinn could locate the missiles, his assignment was to obtain photographic evidence that confirmed their existence and then return. Armed with that proof, the United States and its Caribbean allies could then take unilateral action.

"You're a freaking photographer," Will, his field supervisor, had cautioned. "Get in, and get out."

A flashing white light interrupted Quinn's thoughts. The light was off to his left, some ways away, but bright.

He stopped and kicked in place. It flashed again. A strobe, pulsing.

A muffled droning noise accompanied the flashing light. Some kind of motor, but too high-pitched for a traditional boat engine.

Quinn kicked down to a large rock formation below him and found a hiding spot beneath a craggy overhang. The flashing light headed away from him, toward the other side of the bay. His eyes adjusted and, seconds later, he recognized the shape of the light source.

An AUV, Autonomous Underwater Vehicle. The equivalent of an underwater drone, remotely operated and used for surveillance. This one, shaped like a miniature submarine, stretched about ten feet long. When the light flashed again, Quinn glimpsed the froth from the twin propellers.

It was cruising at about five knots. He was out of range of its camera, whose lens was downward-looking and only photographed what was beneath the drone. And the rock formation would hide him from the drone's sonar.

His hand reflexively touched his holstered HK as he realized how close he'd come to being detected, then, inevitably, captured and interrogated. This Calderon was a man who took pains to guard his secrets.

Quinn kicked on, immersed in his thoughts. Around him,

the Caribbean gradually morphed from monochromatic black to shades of blue, then turquoise. The moon had emerged from behind the clouds, increasing visibility in these shallower waters.

Brightly colored fish—blue tang, glasseye snapper, striped parrotfish—swam all around him, intent on going somewhere and seemingly oblivious to his presence. He kicked past a school of queen angelfish, shimmering in brilliant blue and yellow. Below him lay a large rock formation, draped with honey-gold starfish and purple sea anemones. A lump of dark green seaweed floated next to him, almost within reach, its strands waving in the current.

He gave the seaweed a second glance. Something looked out of place.

He froze when he recognized the black cable, almost invisible, that tethered the seaweed to the ocean floor. A moored contact mine disguised to blend in with the marine life, waiting for an unauthorized vessel. Or a careless diver.

Very clever. What else did Calderon have in his bag of tricks? He cursed to himself and kicked away, past a school of innocent damselfish.

His heart rate picked up when the screen on his dive computer flashed blue, alerting him that the target was three hundred yards away. Two hundred. One hundred.

The outline of a black shape—large, rectangular, and as big as a small building—came into view ahead of him. Acutely aware of how heavily guarded the coastline was, Quinn descended a few more feet and slowed his kick as he approached.

The object became clearer. He could make out a half-circle

atop the rectangle. The half-circle was the dome on top of the silo.

The Giant Wave missiles were there.

Quinn pedaled in place and unstrapped his dive light. Sweeping right to left, he scanned the structure. As he had guessed, the LED beam reflected off a wall of chain-link steel. Indicator nets hung like metal curtains on all sides of the silo.

He kicked closer, inspecting the netting. There. Every twenty feet or so, round steel motion sensors clung to the netting, ready to send an alarm in the event of an intruder.

From a belt pocket, Quinn removed a mesh bag containing small clasps resembling alligator clips. Moving slowly so as to not activate the sensors, he attached the clips bordering an area five-foot square.

Next he removed a pair of bolt-cutters from another pocket and, after a slight tug to ensure the sensors wouldn't detect the movement, he cut out an area of chain-link netting large enough to swim through. The piece of netting sank to the ocean floor.

So far, so good. He put the bolt-cutters away and kicked through the opening.

Next to the silo sat giant cylindrical tanks with tubes connecting to the silo. Probably compressed air, needed for the underwater launch. He removed his Olympus camera and took video of the entire apparatus.

Then he kicked close to the tanks and took still pictures, zooming in for close-ups of the tubes and gauges. Finally, he kicked away and took wide-angle shots of the entire structure.

In ten minutes, he'd videoed the entire silo and taken over fifty photographs. He scrolled through them in the LCD screen. The video resolution was grainy, but the close-up stills showed plenty of incriminating detail in high definition.

The silo was, he had to admit, an impressive feat of engineering. It reinforced his notion that Calderon was no tinhorn. He intended to use these missiles.

Time to get out. The camera snapped securely back into its case.

He kicked through the opening and ascended to fifteen feet. With his compass, he set a straight-line course for the tip of the cove and the waiting Zodiac. He focused on keeping his kick steady, his breathing relaxed. On dive missions, speed kills.

Soon the silo disappeared behind him. The moon still glowed above, and exotic fish swam everywhere in the luminous waters. He was on his way home and allowed himself the luxury of noticing the beauty of the sea life. A school of black-banded butterflyfish cruised in front of him, scattering a group of bright yellow trumpetfish headed in the other direction.

Something hummed to his left. Faint vibrations penetrated his wetsuit. The noise was unmistakable. This time it wasn't the AUV. It was the drone of a boat engine.

He had to see what it was. It sounded far enough away that the risk of his being spotted was minimal. As he kicked up, he reminded himself to keep the look short.

Engine noise reverberated across the water as his facemask broke the surface. Quinn's heart hammered his chest when he saw the boat.

It was a harbor police patrol boat. He could make out the red paint of the *Patrulla de Agua Rica* against the weather-beaten white side of the boat and the shadowy figures of two, maybe three, uniformed men standing on deck. The boat cruised through the bay, and the powerful searchlight atop the cabin made large, lazy circles on the water.

He ducked below the surface.

The harbor patrol boat was making a wide loop around the entire cove. Probably a routine patrol, in case intruders were foolish enough to approach from the open sea.

The engine boomed through the water. The damned boat was passing right in front of him. Would its searchlight reach him?

He reached for his BCD valve. All he had to do was descend and make a slight detour underneath the boat's wake. His rebreather left no telltale trail of bubbles. The men onboard had no inkling of his existence. They were probably talking about where to get a drink after their shift.

The detour would consume precious time, but it was the only option.

The water around him had grown murky. Odd little things floated in it. Debris from the boat?

Oily gunk stuck to his mask. He reached up with his glove and cleared it away, but the stuff still smeared on his mask and stuck to his glove.

Something bumped into his left shoulder. Then a series of small punches buffeted him on the right. From above, something banged into his facemask then whisked away.

He whirled around. Everywhere he looked, the water churned. Flashes of silver streaked in every direction. Larger fish—tuna, bass, grouper—surrounded him, darting crazily every which way, as if they'd gone mad.

He brought his glove up to his facemask and looked at the

stuff sticking to it. Fish guts. In the moonlight, he could see the water around him tinted a faint red.

The boat had been spraying chum and blood on the water as it cruised by, in order to create a feeding frenzy.

And he was in the middle of it.

Something tugged hard at his right fin tip. He shook his leg free and brought his foot up. A chunk of his fin tip was gone.

Next to his foot swam two silver, bullet-shaped fish, perhaps three-feet long.

Barracuda.

One of the barracuda opened its scissors-like jaws to an almost ninety-degree angle, showing off its razor-sharp teeth, and spat out the piece of black fin tip. The two barracuda eyed Quinn as if deciding where to strike next.

He backpedaled, pulled out his knife, and lunged forward. He screamed inside his dive mask, trying to scare away the barracuda.

The fish darted to the sides then regrouped, joined by more. Now a half-dozen barracuda clustered in front of him.

Quinn sweated profusely inside his wetsuit. Calderon had thought of everything. Stock the bay with marine predators, then drive them to be even more aggressive with the bloodlust of feeding frenzies. A modern-day equivalent of crocodiles in the moat, and so much simpler than having to locate an intruder and drop depth charges.

If a boat were foolish enough to launch a diver into this bay, the clean-picked human bones, which would wash up on some distant shore, would bear no trace of any crime.

He couldn't possibly outrun the barracuda, and his retreat

would be interpreted as weakness. He lashed out with his knife again, screaming at the top of his lungs. This time the barracuda scattered and quickly reformed their pack.

He tried to remember something of barracuda behavior that would give him an edge. They were voracious carnivores, their aggression compounded by blood in the water.

A flash of silver broke from the side of the pack as one of the barracuda darted forward, its gaping jaws showing its fang-like teeth. Quinn ducked, and the barracuda's teeth glanced off his dive tank with a *clang*.

He brought his head up, waving his knife wildly in front of him. He'd been lucky that time. Any second now, there would be another flash of silver. Teeth would slash through his wetsuit, and cold seawater would ooze in as the barracuda ripped a chunk of flesh away from his leg or his arm. And as soon as his blood drifted into the water, the rest of the pack would be on him.

The barracuda regrouped in front of him.

Quinn startled as a large black shape loomed in the corner of his eye.

The black shape surged into the center of the pack. The pack of barracuda scattered. The shape's jaws snapped shut on a barracuda that was a hair too slow.

The barracuda's head flopped wildly back and forth. The jaws of the black shape opened and closed again, and the severed head of the barracuda floated away, its jaws perma-nently open, trailing blood.

Quinn stayed still, his knife held in front of him. Maybe the black shape would move on, looking for other fish.

The shape swam toward the surface, and in the moonlight,

Quinn glimpsed a white underbelly and a row of dark stripes on a massive blue-green body. The large dorsal fin on top was the clincher.

It was a tiger shark, about ten feet long.

Quinn cursed as his mind went into overdrive.

The tiger shark was king in these waters, a fearless hunter with a keen sense of smell. What the hell would this one do in a sea of blood?

Despite the chum in the water, all the other fish had vanished. Their survival instinct overruled their feeding frenzy. Now the shark, supreme ruler of this cove, lazily turned around and swam down and back to Quinn's right, in the direction it had come, as if it had all the time in the world.

He stayed motionless. Perhaps the shark would think he was just a floating mass of driftwood and seaweed. If he kept still, it would pass him by.

But its head turned for a closer look, and its cold, black eye stared at him. Its ugly grey snout turned toward him like some sort of battering ram.

His knife would be useless against the hurtling thousand-pound creature. Quinn slipped it back in its sheath and wrapped his hand around the butt of his HK. It would be his only chance. He held his breath and stayed still.

The shark hung motionless in the water, sizing him up. Then its great tail whipped, and it shot right at him.

He ducked down and to the right, bringing up his HK. The shark's mouth opened into a huge black oval with rows of serrated white teeth.

Quinn fired all five rounds in quick succession—two

181

projectiles at the big left eye and the remaining three as deep as he could into the creature's gaping maw.

He ducked down and kicked away for his life, expecting the massive jaws to crush his lower back. Instead, a force knocked him sideways with tremendous turbulence. He righted himself and looked up.

He'd hit his mark. Streams of black mist poured from the shark's mouth and eye. Its body thrashed, and its jaws opened and closed in violent spasms.

Then the shark's remaining eye noticed him. The jaws shut. Its snout turned in his direction, preparing for another strike.

Quinn backpedaled. The HK pistol was spent. He holstered it. All he had left to fight with was his knife. He pulled it out of its sheath and held it in front of him. His best chance was to get the blade into the shark's other eye.

Silver glinted to his right. The silver streak flashed forward, lightning fast, and attacked the shark. It backed away slowly, a large chunk of flesh dangling in its jaws. Black mist poured out of a fist-sized gouge in the shark's flank.

The barracuda had returned.

Two more barracuda shot in like streaks of silver, and more black clouds appeared alongside the shark.

Something in the primeval DNA of predators received signals when prey was vulnerable, when it was defenseless and exposed. The wounded shark, as formidable as it had once been, had now become prey.

The weakened shark turned toward its enemies to fight back but was too slow.

The entire pack of barracuda descended like mad dogs on

the shark, tearing chunks of flesh out of its grey snout, its white belly, everywhere.

Quinn turned and kicked away from the grisly scene. The patrol boat would still be headed on its loop toward the side of the cove. This was his window of opportunity to escape before the boat doubled back.

He checked his compass and kicked toward the tip of the cove.

Breathe, kick. Breathe, kick. His arms ached, his thighs burned, and fish caromed off him, but he put it all out of his mind and focused on staying the course. Gradually the bits and pieces of chum dispersed, and the fish receded into the background.

The drone of the patrol boat faded until the only noise was his own breathing in the regulator. His heartbeat slowed to normal, and the clammy sweat dried and stuck to his body. Around him, the ink-black sea had calmed once more, parting in front of him as he swam.

To his right, the sight of jagged rocks signaled his proximity to the tip of the cove. He pressed the valve of his BCD and ascended to about ten feet below the surface.

Above him, moonlight shone on the barren rock. He kicked on, staying clear of the rocks as he rounded the tip of the cove.

Relief surged through his veins at the wonderful sight of the Zodiac, bobbing with the sea, waiting where it had dropped him off. Quinn kicked the last several yards to the side of the boat and surfaced.

O'Donnell stood in the boat, wearing a worried look on his face as he peered at the blood and fragments of fish guts clinging to Quinn's mask and suit. "What the hell happened out there?"

Quinn slipped off his mask and mouthpiece and took a few gulps of real air.

"Unexpected company. But…" He unclasped his rebreather and felt the weight of the unit slip off his chest.

Above him, the clouds had cleared to a jet-black sky. Stars glittered around a brilliant moon.

He had never felt so happy just to be alive.

"Mission accomplished."

THE BALLERINA

A MICHAEL QUINN SHORT STORY

KEVIN SCOTT OLSON

There is a history in all men's lives…

— SHAKESPEARE

THE BALLERINA

Laguna Beach, California

LAGUNA BEACH, ON AN APRIL AFTERNOON, WAS THE sleepy little beach town it should always be.

Michael Quinn slowed his BMW to a stop at a red light and savored the familiar beauty of one of his favorite places in the world.

Couples, young and old, held hands and sipped coffee at outdoor cafés. Tanned women in shorts and sandals gazed into boutique windows, and tanned men with backpacks and surfboards gazed at the women.

The rainy winter had turned the hills on his left a lush green. To his right, the Pacific Ocean rippled steel blue against a beach of immaculate golden sand.

The stoplight changed. Quinn drove through the winding, picturesque streets of town and onto an empty stretch of Pacific Coast Highway.

The mystery lay ahead, between the hills and the sea.

His destination, the Montage Laguna Beach, came up on his right. He slowed as he turned off the highway and onto the hotel's long driveway, dappled from the sun shining through the trees.

The mystery came from the text he had received that morning. The words, synched from his cell phone to his BMW's dashboard display, still glared on the screen.

The Director is in town and would like to meet with you tonight. Dinner at 1800 hours sharp. Montage, the Admiralty Room. Business attire.

Short and sweet, that text. Yet those few words were about to lead him into uncharted territory.

Due to the nature of his assignments and his status as an independent contractor, Michael Quinn could never be overtly connected in any way with the Central Intelligence Agency. Meeting anyone at Langley was thus out of the question.

His briefings with the CIA Director were invariably held at Foxfield, the Director's secluded ranch in the Virginia country-side. He was never to meet with the Director anyplace else.

Until, apparently, now.

Why?

Quinn pulled up under the portico and handed his keys to the valet. He put on his blue blazer which, together with gray slacks and a burgundy tie, formed his default "business attire," and strode through the columned entrance into the hotel.

Down the main hallway, just before the piano lounge, two men in coats and ties stood guard in front of a quiet side hallway that led only to the Admiralty Room. They chatted amiably, trying to blend in as hotel guests, but their discreet earpieces and the slight bulge from their shoulder holsters belied their innocence.

They fell silent and nodded in recognition as Quinn walked up to them.

A flaxen-haired hostess waited for him at the entrance to the Admiralty Room. She was elegant in a cream silk blouse and black pencil skirt, and she smiled as she opened the double doors.

The Director stood at the head of a dining table large enough to seat twenty.

"Good evening, Michael. Thank you for coming on short notice." Fit and fiftyish, he wore his usual navy suit, white shirt, and red military-striped tie.

"Evening, Director." Quinn shook hands.

The Director gestured at the man standing next to him. "I'd like to introduce you to a friend. Brandon Lloyd, of Lloyd and Charles."

Lloyd and Charles was a high-end auction house, head-quartered in London, specializing in rare art and jewelry. What was this all about?

Quinn turned to the other man and extended his hand. "Nice to meet you, sir."

Brandon Lloyd, sixtyish and silver-haired in a charcoal pinstripe suit, looked him over with polite curiosity as they shook hands. "A distinct pleasure, Mr. Quinn."

The Director pulled his chair back. "Gentlemen, please be seated. Shannon, here, will take your orders."

They made small talk as the hostess passed out menus.

The Admiralty Room was a nautical-themed private dining room with oil paintings of great sailing ships displayed above mahogany wainscoting. The entire far wall was a picture window with a spectacular view of the Pacific. In late afternoon, the sea had turned a battleship gray, and the sun melted to blood red at the horizon.

The Director motioned at the window. "I see why you like to come here, Michael. Since we're on your turf, do you have any recommendations for appetizers? My English friend, here, fancies himself an epicurean."

"Well, their *maître fromager* is world-class, sir."

Brandon nodded in approval, and the Director picked up the wine list. "Then we'll take you at your word."

The hostess took their orders and left the room.

The Director glanced at his phone and sat back in his chair. "We have a lot to cover, so let's get to the matter at hand. One of our key sources lives here in Laguna Beach. He has extensive contacts around the world and has been of considerable assistance to us over the years."

"Assistance" could mean a thousand different things. The Director defaulted to bland verbiage as necessary, more so when a third party was present.

He paused as he chose his next words. "This source is also an old friend. I was best man at his wedding, twenty-five years ago. He's had a good run since then. After making a small fortune with his import-export business, he sold his company and retired, concentrating his energies on his passion for collecting artworks."

The Director glanced out the window. "Recent times have not been so kind. His wife passed away a couple of years back, and he became a recluse, living alone with his art collection.

For the past few weeks he's been hospitalized with multiple health issues. Kept it all to himself.

"Now things have taken a turn for the worse. So much so that he declined further treatment and went home to live out his days. That's when he called me."

Quinn leaned forward, sensing that the phone call lay behind this meeting.

The Director continued. "We met with him last night. Beautiful home, in the hills. He's putting his affairs in order and made a request that I promised I would honor." He looked at Quinn. "It is time-sensitive. That's why I asked you here tonight. Your calendar has been cleared for the next several days, correct?"

"It has, sir."

The Director's phone buzzed. He texted a response, and the two guards ushered in the hostess with their drinks and the white-hatted *fromager*, a twenty-something man carrying a silver tray with an array of cheeses and compotes.

The hostess set down their drinks. Her blonde hair brushed Quinn's shoulder as she put his glass of whiskey on a coaster. He caught a glimpse of inquiring blue eyes, and then she briskly walked out of the room.

The *fromager* lingered, hovering over the tray with the passion of an artist as he explained the assortment of cheeses, from the aged Gouda to the rare Spanish Manchego. When he finished, the security detail politely escorted him from the room and closed the door behind them.

The Director sipped his cabernet and selected a piece of goat cheese. "This assignment is about a hunt for missing treasure—one item, in particular. Brandon will fill you in on the details."

"Mr. Quinn, are you familiar with the Fabergé eggs?" Brandon Lloyd removed a tablet computer from his briefcase and placed it on the table.

"A little." Quinn sipped his Glenfiddich single malt on-the-rocks. "They were artworks made for the Russian royal family over a century ago, during the days of Imperial Russia. Their artistry is legendary."

"Quite right." Lloyd spoke with the polished elocution of the auctioneer. "The House of Fabergé, court jeweler to the royal family, was commissioned to make them. These small, egg-shaped objects rank among the world's finest artworks.

"They were made each Easter. At the beginning of spring, after the dark and cold Russian winter, these eggs symbolized life itself and became a beloved tradition.

"Just a few inches in length and beautifully decorated on the outside, each egg is also hinged to open. Inside is the 'surprise,' a superb work of craftsmanship made of gold and silver and the finest gemstones. Words can't do them justice, though." He pressed a button on the side of the tablet computer.

The high-definition screen sprang to life, sparkling with jeweled objects of stunning color and design. The first egg was the pale green of emerald, draped in gold garlands. Then came a royal blue egg shimmering with pearls. Both opened up to reveal intricate figurines dazzling with diamonds, sapphires, and rubies.

"Today, most of the eggs are accounted for. The Queen of England has three, as part of the Royal Collection. The

Kremlin Museum has several. Most of the rest are in private hands. Fewer than sixty Fabergé eggs survive in the world, and they are quite valuable. Each piece is now worth millions of dollars.

"However, there are a few Fabergé eggs still missing after all these years. Of those, the one that is regarded as the most beautiful, and perhaps the most valuable of all, is called 'The Ballerina.'

"'The Ballerina' was made for the Danilova family. They were prominent Russian nobility, with a family mansion and considerable wealth." Lloyd swiped the tablet screen, and it showed an old black-and-white photograph of a Russian family.

The family was gathered on a clear day in a formal garden with roses and sculpted junipers. They stood in two concentric semicircles. Behind them towered an elegant, neo-classical mansion with six tall columns. The men wore full dress uniform, with braids and medals, and the women wore elaborate gowns.

"They were a handsome family." Brandon Lloyd sighed as he looked at the photograph. "But back to this Fabergé egg created for them. It was made out of the finest white gold.

"The top of the egg displayed a lily, made of emerald and pearl, symbolizing spring. The Danilova daughters were famed ballerinas, and so this gift had a ballerina inside as its 'surprise,' surrounded by the melting snow and ice of spring, all beautifully done in white gold, pearls, and diamonds. 'The Ballerina' became the family's prize heirloom."

Quinn waited for a photograph of "The Ballerina" to show on the screen.

Instead, Brandon Lloyd touched the screen, and it went dark. His voice lowered. "Unfortunately, the Danilova family, along with the rest of Russian royalty, lost everything when the Communists took over in 1918."

Another photo filled the screen. It was of a vacant lot with mounds of rocks and dirt under a hazy sky.

Quinn startled when he recognized the bottom shape of six of the mounds. They were all that remained of the columns of the mansion in the previous photograph.

This photograph was taken from the exact same point of view as the previous photo, but now all of the people were gone. The garden was gone, and scarred, seared earth replaced the roses and junipers. Everything was gone. The vacant lot on a hazy day was the smoking ruins of the Danilova family home.

Brandon Lloyd continued. "Their mansion was ransacked and burned to the ground, as you can see here. Many of the family members you saw in that first photograph were executed. All of the family valuables, all of their wealth and property, were taken. The Danilova family never recovered and faded into obscurity."

"And 'The Ballerina?'" Quinn stared at the ruins.

"Vanished."

"And no one has seen this piece since? Are there photographs?"

"Not even a drawing. Just rumors from all over. One is that a desperate Stalin sold it to raise cash for his starving Soviet Union. Another is that it was dropped at night into the Black Sea."

"That doesn't leave much to go on." Quinn sipped his

whiskey.

"Until last night." The Director spoke up. "When we met with our source, he took us to a walk-in vault next to his wine cellar. In there, on magnificent display, was 'The Ballerina.' Brandon verified its authenticity."

"No doubt, whatsoever." Brandon Lloyd sipped his wine. "It is unforgettable."

The room went silent for a moment. Quinn wondered, *if you've found it, then why do you need me?*

The Director glanced out the window. The blood-red sun was fading to black at the horizon, and the evening's first stars shone high in the sky. "There is one surviving member of the Danilova family. A woman named Elena Danilova." He looked at Quinn. "Our source wants 'The Ballerina' to be passed on to her."

Asked and answered. The vague shape of a mission formed in Quinn's mind. "And what do we know about this Elena?"

Brandon Lloyd leaned forward and swiped the screen of his tablet. The old black-and-white photo of ruins was replaced by a bright, color video of a striking young woman.

She was a ballerina, clothed all in white, dancing the lead on a stage decorated to look like a lake in a forest. Her diamond tiara sparkled atop blonde hair in a bun.

The ballerina leaped high in the air, her athletic legs rippling with curves, and landed with precision and poise. She held the pose, her arms spread out like wings, breathing hard as the audience stood and applauded.

Quinn looked closer. Her facial features were delicate and pretty, with high, curved cheekbones and large, aquamarine eyes. "She's beautiful. But this looks like old 16 mm film."

"It is precisely that, Mr. Quinn." Brandon Lloyd watched the video. "It is about sixty years old. Elena was a promising ballerina back then, a rising star. But an injury cut her career short when she was still in her twenties. With no other skills, she became a government clerk.

"And just another might-have been. Never married, no children, no money." Lloyd's finger lingered over the screen. "Now she's pretty much forgotten, an old woman living in a humble apartment in Saint Petersburg, Russia. Here is a picture of her now." He swiped the screen.

It showed a color photo, probably taken from a cell phone, of an elderly woman, walking down the sidewalk of a down-scale street in winter. She wore a thick overcoat, a scarf on her gray-haired head, and she carried two shopping bags. The woman looked down at the sidewalk as she walked.

Quinn studied her wrinkled facial features and matched them to those of the ballerina. "I suppose a direct bequest to her from this gentleman's will is not an option?"

The Director placed his glass on the table. "Michael, our source has never disclosed to anyone that he is the owner of this artwork. He wouldn't even let us photograph it last night."

Brandon Lloyd leaned forward. "Allow me to explain. Most private owners of such pieces take great care to remain anonymous. Not just for tax or insurance reasons. It is for their own physical safety.

"Mr. Quinn, your United States is one of the few countries in the world where a wealthy man can walk around without armed guards. But even here, just owning such a valuable item can put your life in danger.

"Collectors thus use auction houses, such as ours, to act as buyers, to protect their identity when they bid on an item. And they then go to great lengths to stay unknown."

The Director tapped his fingers together. "Moreover, the Russian mafia is extremely active at the high levels of the art world. We've run into them before. They would do anything to get their hands on a piece that is so immensely valuable, not to mention a part of Russian history."

Quinn downed the rest of his whiskey and let its cold fire burn in his stomach. "So the mission is to make sure one of the most valuable artworks in the world gets to its proper heir. I imagine the firm of Lloyd and Charles is involved?"

The Director nodded. "In three days, a very ostentatious caravan—an armored truck guarded front and back by police escorts and SUVs with armed guards—will drive from the Saint Petersburg office of Lloyd and Charles to a private museum a few miles away. Hints will be dropped, in the right places, that the precious cargo in the armored truck might be the priceless piece known as 'The Ballerina.'"

"A decoy," said Quinn. "Good. And the transfer of the real 'Ballerina?'"

"That's where you come in."

Three days later
Saint Petersburg, Russia

THE SHOPPING CART STOPPED, STUCK IN ANOTHER OF THE cracks that scarred the concrete sidewalk.

Elena Danilova rubbed her wrinkled hands together, sighed, and looked around.

Moyska Street was one of the bleakest streets in Saint Petersburg. The gloomy fog seemed designed to blend with the dreary Soviet-era concrete buildings. Graffiti covered almost every storefront, even the ones open for business. The melting snow of April had turned the grimy gutters into gray-black rivers.

It was a world apart from the beautiful shops and restaurants of Nevsky Prospekt, just a few miles away. Right now, affluent tourists and residents were probably enjoying hot Russian crepes with caviar and mushrooms before going out for an evening at the theater.

But that was not her world. Her tiny apartment overlooked a vacant lot of weeds and broken glass, and the hot water for her building had already been shut off for the season.

She straightened out the shopping cart and pushed it forward.

Across the street, three shorthaired young men hanging out in front of a dingy bar stopped their banter and stared at her. They dressed as hooligans did these days, in black pants, shirts, gloves, and jackets, with the badges of their "fight club" sewn onto their jackets.

Such men were dangerous. These modern-day hooligans, she had heard, trained hard and fought to maim and kill, with knives hidden in their jackets and metal pellets lining their gloves. She stared straight ahead, avoiding eye contact.

One of the hooligans cupped his hands and called her *starukha*—"old woman"—while the others sneered.

Ignore them. She didn't care, anyway.

At the age of eighty-four, she'd long since valued her warm scarf and thick coat more than any sense of fashion. All that mattered to her now was the Church of the Merciful Savior, her beloved church to which she'd devoted her remaining years. That was her world.

The shopping cart's wheels rattled as she turned the corner onto Puschkaya Street. *Only a couple of blocks to go.*

She reminded herself again why she was doing this. She had been told to push the cart to a certain shop in this seedy area of the city. There, she was to offer the contents of the cart, and in exchange she would receive special gifts that she was to take to her church.

If Elena followed these simple instructions, there would be more food for the hungry vagabonds who came to her church's soup kitchen. She didn't know exactly how it would happen, but she'd been assured that it would be worthwhile.

She looked down at the worn, stained blanket that covered the cart's contents. Who on earth would want such junk? It was all castoffs—cheap, secondhand knickknacks that had been sitting in the church basement.

She'd helped run the church's soup kitchen for several years. Even in the best of times, the Church of the Merciful Savior, located in a poorer part of the city, had barely scraped by.

Now, with the recent economic upheavals, there was no money to fix the ancient plumbing or to patch the leaking roof, and those were given priority over the soup kitchen.

Elena did what she could, scrounging from local stores for expired foodstuffs and from restaurants for leftovers. But there was never enough. Every day, it seemed, more downtrodden souls, from the lonely elderly to orphaned children, showed up at the kitchen, hoping for a hot meal.

The shopping cart stopped again as the right front wheel tipped into a crack. She jerked the cart back, straightened it out, and glanced down the street. Thick fog was everywhere, streaming toward her like tentacles. What she could see of the street looked deserted, but she felt like someone was watching her.

She turned around. No one was there. Only a fleeting glimpse of the back end of a black car turning the corner, driving away.

Elena peered through the fog and pushed the cart around a patch of dirty snow. She reflected, as she often did these days, on her long life.

Among her earliest memories was the night her family had fled the Nazi hordes that threatened the entire city. She'd only been a little girl at the time, and they had hidden in a barn on the outskirts of town—without heat or plumbing—and lived for months on bread and water that her mother would whisper to her came from something called the Road of Life.

It was only later, after the war had ended in glorious victory for Russia, that she learned that her family had lived in relative comfort. When she returned to school, she soon discovered why so many of her childhood friends never came back. They and their families had starved to death during the siege.

Elena pushed the cart forward, her breath forming white plumes in the frigid air. She would soon reach her destination. Her mind searched for happier memories.

The best years of her life were as a dancer. As a child, after seeing a performance of "Swan Lake," she told her parents she wanted more than anything to be a ballerina.

They were aware of the family history of ballerinas and somehow found money for ballet school. By her teenage years, she was attracting attention from ballet companies, and as a young woman, she blossomed into a *prima ballerina*, a principal dancer with the St. Petersburg Ballet. There was talk of going on tour, maybe to the West.

The knee injury ended all of that at the age of twenty-two.

Fortunately, she'd found a steady job as a city clerk. The hours were long and the pay was low, but she had food to eat and a place to live. She got by.

From then on, the years blurred together. From the Soviet Union to the Russian Federation, little had changed in her life, except that under Communism, she'd been forced to hide her faith. People were persecuted and arrested for simply attending church services. These days, the State left her free to devote her life to her faith.

Just the thought of her church lifted her spirits. Her favorite sight in the world was the magnificent array of globes atop the church. They were painted gold, blue, and green, and they reached up and beckoned to the heavens. Some said the colors represented the Holy Trinity; others said they represented candles that burned for eternity.

She thought of the church's beautiful paintings of the saints, of the painting of the Mother of God with Child, and of the entire interior wall devoted to a striking mosaic of Christ giving a blessing. Surely it was a miracle that her beautiful church had survived the war intact.

She shuddered in the cold, despite her thick coat. The fog

seemed to be closing in. She had to get back to the church before dark. At night, these streets were no place for an old woman.

Elena's thoughts lingered on her age, her mortality. Soon her generation would fade away into history.

She knew from what she saw on television and in the press that a new generation of wealthy Russians now ran her country. These men had mansions with fleets of expensive cars and villas in Switzerland and Italy. They dined on sushi and sipped the finest vodka while consorting with mistresses and girlfriends who could've been cover models on magazines.

They were nothing like the dull Party *nomenklatura* of the old days. This generation seemed to have unlimited wealth, and they did what they pleased with it.

Elena didn't understand how this could be, but she didn't care. She was at peace with her life and her faith.

A car engine growled from behind her, and she turned around to see a black car cruising down the street. It looked like the car she'd seen driving away earlier.

It wasn't a Mercedes or a Bentley like one might see on Nevsky Prospekt. The car was an old black Lada with a heavyset man at the wheel. It passed her, turned the corner, and vanished into the fog.

The shopping cart squeaked to a halt. She had reached her destination. The one-story brick building lay between an empty laundromat and a shuttered store. The faded sign above the entry read, "Petrushkin and Company."

Elena had never been to a pawnshop. Their clientele, presumably, were people with valuable assets who were in need of quick cash. Maybe she would see fine gold watches and diamond jewelry.

She opened the glass entry door and pushed her cart inside.

This shop apparently catered to the working class. A solitary display case stood in the center of the store. A meager assortment of cheap watches and costume jewelry lay on faded black velvet inside the case. Floor-to-ceiling rows of shelves crammed with books, clothing, and household items filled the rest of the store.

"*Dobryi den, moya dorogaya.*" The polite greeting came from a potbellied old man wearing suspenders and a T-shirt that looked as if he'd slept in it. Tufts of white hair bookended his pink, bald pate, and his jowly face showed a kindly grin.

He walked slowly out from behind the back counter, bowed, and looked appraisingly at the cart.

"*Dobryi den.*" Elena, not quite sure what to do next, gestured toward the cart.

"At your service, madam. And what have we here?" He lifted back the blanket.

"These are things from our church basement, sir. I was told to bring them here."

"Really? Let's have a look."

The man removed a set of scuffed *matryoshka* nesting dolls depicting young girls in peasant costumes, some dinnerware, pots and pans, and several articles of old clothing. He piled everything on the counter and looked at her.

"Did you wish to pawn these items or sell them?"

"Sell or trade, sir." She had rehearsed her line carefully.

The man raised his hands. "I can give you nothing in the

way of rubles. These things are worth next to nothing. But I know you from the church. Perhaps I can let you take some things in trade as goodwill. What do you need?"

"Our church houses many homeless during the winter. Perhaps bedding?"

"Of course."

The man walked over to the dusty shelves behind the back counter and looked them up and down. After a moment, he bent over and pulled out three wool blankets and three large pillows.

Carefully, he placed them on the counter. The blankets were old but looked clean and in good shape. The pillows looked almost new.

"Will these help, my lady?"

"Yes."

The man placed the items in her shopping cart and covered it with her worn blanket.

"I'm happy we can help, sister. "

"Thank you, sir. " Elena put her hands on the shopping cart handle and turned to leave.

"Just a moment." The old man raised his voice.

Elena's heart fluttered. Had she done something wrong?

"The day is getting late. The streets are not safe. You need an escort back to your church." The old man turned and pulled aside a curtain that covered the entry to the back room of the pawnshop just enough to poke his head in.

Then the old man stepped back, the curtain moved, and a young man, much younger than the proprietor, walked out from the back room of the pawnshop. He was dressed in jeans, boots, and a leather jacket.

The old man smiled. "This is my assistant, Mikhail. He will be happy to walk you back to your church."

"Oh! It is not necessary, sir." Elena's hands trembled as she gripped the cart. No one had mentioned this.

"I insist, my lady. Mikhail, if you please?"

"*Dobryi den,*" the young man spoke politely.

She looked him over. He was *krasivyy,* handsome, with brown hair and blue eyes. He looked strong and fit as he walked past and held the door open for her. His manners were those of a gentleman. Her instincts told her he was trustworthy.

Perhaps it was a good idea after all. She nodded at the shopkeeper.

"If you insist, sir. *Do svidaniya.*"

"*Do svidaniya, spasibo.*" The old man watched as Elena pushed her cart out onto the sidewalk.

Mikhail closed the door behind them and insisted on pushing her shopping cart for her. She felt awkward, but he made pleasant small talk as they walked side by side. After half a block, she was more comfortable with him. He seemed genuinely interested in her, almost as if he knew who she was.

Don't fool yourself. You are an old woman, and no one cares. It just had been a long time since she'd been in the company of such a handsome young man.

She stole glances at him as they made their way toward the church. He looked about thirty, athletic, and pushed the cart with ease. His eyes were warm and friendly when they looked at her, but cold when they scanned the street in front of them. She sensed he had an acute awareness of his surroundings.

He was not Russian; she was certain of that. He spoke the

language well enough, and his grammar was correct, but his inflections gave him away. He occasionally stressed the wrong syllable in a word, the way Westerners do. He was American, or maybe English.

So how had he ended up working in a Russian pawnshop?

Another thing seemed out of place. Every few minutes, Mikhail checked his cell phone. What was so important about being a pawn shop clerk?

Elena glimpsed the phone screen once, and it showed video of some sort of armored truck driving down Nevsky Prospekt, with police cars and large black vehicles driving in front and in back. The light bars on the police cars flashed blue and white. Something important was happening on the other side of town.

They turned a corner, and Mikhail put his cell phone back in his pocket and smiled at her. Now it was only two more blocks to her church.

Most of the shops had closed now, and the first streetlights glowed in the mist. The black Lada drove by again. Mikhail watched as it slowed almost to a stop, then it turned the corner and was gone.

"Elena, have you seen that car before?"

"Why, yes. It passed me on the way over."

The hooligans still lingered out in front of the bar, but now they were talking with a group of tattooed girls. The hooligans stared at Elena and Mikhail as they walked by. She felt Mikhail scrutinizing them.

"And those men, Elena. Were they there, in front of the bar, on your way over?"

"Yes, but they are just local ruffians. I ignored them."

Mikhail now seemed preoccupied. He was still polite but less focused on her and more on their surroundings. When she made conversation, his replies were short, almost abrupt. He looked behind them as they turned the corner to the last block.

They walked the rest of the way in silence. The street was empty and quiet. They reached the church at twilight, but the low fog hid what was left of the sun and turned everything as gray as the concrete all around them.

A wrought-iron fence surrounded the church, and its large entry gate hung open. Concrete steps led from the gate up to the church's tall wooden doors. The steps each spanned several feet in length but only a few inches in height so the elderly churchgoers could climb them.

Mikhail lifted the cart wheels over the first step and then pushed the cart toward the second step.

He stopped halfway, his head turning at the roar of a car engine and the screech of tires coming to a sudden stop.

The black Llada had pulled up right in front of the entry gate. The heavyset man was at the wheel.

Elena's heart pounded when she saw the three hooligans climb out of the car. Black balaclavas now covered their faces, making them look like Grim Reapers. They jogged at a brisk pace toward the church gate.

"Elena," Mikhail's voice was harsh as he grabbed her hands and placed them on the shopping cart handle. "These are bad men. I will stop them, but I need you to push the cart the rest of the way until it is safely inside the church. Do you understand? Go!"

He was already jogging down the steps as she nodded yes.

Her hands trembled, and the cart seemed heavy, but she pushed it up the next step, and then the step after that. What was this? What did those young men want with her?

She risked a look back. The three hooligans surrounded Mikhail, who stood at the gate opening with his back to her. One hooligan faced him straight on, and the other two were circling to his right and left.

"Elena, go!" yelled Mikhail, as if he knew she had looked back.

Her hands shook and her breath came hard as she shoved the cart up what now seemed like a steep hill. Two long steps to go.

In front of her, the church entry door cracked open. Someone inside must have heard the noises. Behind her, the hooligans shouted curses, and then the shouting stopped, replaced by grunts and thumping sounds.

The cart reached the last step. The church door opened wide, and the florid face of the white-haired priest peeked out. He motioned for Elena to hurry, then he grabbed the front of the shopping cart and pulled it over the threshold and into the church foyer.

The noises behind her stopped. As the priest closed the door, Elena turned for another look outside.

Two of the hooligans lay on the ground, one on his back and one on his side. Both lay completely still. The third was on his knees. Mikhail was bent over him and had his arms around the man's neck.

Mikhail bent the man forward, toward the ground. The man's arms flailed, and then weakened, until they collapsed as he went limp. Mikhail laid him down on his side and then released his grip. The man lay still, as if asleep.

Tires screeched as the black Llada abruptly pulled away from the curb. The Llada vanished into the fog as the church doors closed with a solid double-click.

The priest locked the door and then secured the deadbolts as well. He rolled the cart into the foyer, then motioned for Elena to unload its contents.

She shook the blankets, then folded them and laid them on a side table. Then, as she'd been instructed, she lifted up the pillows one by one. The third one was heavier.

She reached inside the pillowcase, and removed a small metal box with the lid securely taped shut. The tape yielded to her fingers, and the lid opened. Inside, wrapped in foam rubber, was a small, egg-shaped object.

It was an Easter egg. *All of this effort for a child's toy?*

She placed it on a wood table in the center of the foyer, under the light of the chandelier.

The egg seemed to glow with a soft sheen, as if it had somehow come to life, and the top glistened green and pinkish white. She looked closer.

The entire egg was made of white gold. A finely sculpted lily decorated the top. The lily stem was carved from emerald, and the flower was iridescent pearl.

Memories from long ago stirred in Elena's mind. Stories she had been told as a child, by her parents and grandparents, of a time when the Danilova family lived a fairy-tale life of nobility. And of the most precious family heirloom from that time, a jeweled artwork.

Her fingers felt the metal hinge at the back of the egg. She grasped the top of the egg with her thumb and forefinger and lifted.

Tears ran down her wrinkled face as she gazed at the beautiful little ballerina, dressed all in white, centered inside. Carved entirely out of white gold, with a diamond tiara, the dancer was surrounded by melting snow made from glistening pearls. Tiny diamonds—thousands of them, more than she'd ever imagined—sparkled everywhere as ice crystals, winter's remnant giving way to spring.

Her bony fingers caressed the shimmering stones. She was transfixed in admiration of their sheer beauty. But the world this glittering treasure came from had never been her world and never would be.

Chills went down her spine as she realized the enormity of this gift. It was hers. But it wasn't really hers. It had been given to her for a higher purpose.

A wealthy collector would provide "The Ballerina" a good home, and in exchange, her church would receive more money than she had ever dreamed possible—enough to make all repairs and improvements, enough to provide sustenance to all of the needy souls that came to its door.

Surely, this was a miracle. A miracle that "The Ballerina" had crossed her path, and a miracle that it would transform her life and the lives of those around her. For all this and more, her aged heart ached with gratitude.

Movement flickered in her peripheral vision, and she glanced out one of the church's windows in time to see Mikhail walking away from the church.

He headed down an alley perpendicular to the street. Then he disappeared into the fog blanketing the city.

BREAKOUT

A Michael Quinn Short Story

Kevin Scott Olson

I have a special relationship with death.

— BRANDON WEBB

BREAKOUT

Prisión Federal Norte Baja
Mexico

"YOU WANT TO EAT TONIGHT, *GRINGO?*"

The prison guard lifted the plastic bowl off the tray and set the tray on the floor. He held the bowl out in front of him, displaying its contents—a watery brown liquid with a few beans floating on top.

"You can have your dinner. All it takes is a little *mordida*. A little of this." The guard rubbed his thumb against the fingers of his free hand in a folding-money motion. His pock-marked brown face creased into a yellow-toothed smile.

The prisoner sat, hunched over, on the edge of his bunk. He glanced at the bowl then stared at the concrete floor of his cell and spoke softly. "Already told you boys. Ain't got no more money."

The black-uniformed guard sighed. His smile disappeared, and he glanced at the guard standing next to him. The other guard shrugged and silently chewed his toothpick, one hand resting on the butt of his holstered pistol.

"That is not good for you, my friend. No, not good." The prison guard gestured at the cramped cell, furnished solely with a filth-encrusted open toilet, a sink, and a metal bunk. "You can have better than this. Everything you might want, it is for sale in this prison.

"You want a cell with a window?" he pointed at the concrete wall. "Maybe pizza? Drugs? A pretty *puta* to keep you company at night? You got money, you can have all those things.

"But with no money... " The guard bent over, holding the bowl level with the prisoner's face. He stared until the prisoner looked up and made eye contact. Then the guard hawked and spat into the bowl. "...you get this."

The guard tilted the bowl, and the brown liquid poured onto the prisoner's shoes.

"*Damn you!*" The prisoner's manacled right fist lashed out, landing a solid uppercut to the guard's jaw.

The bowl flew across the room, and the guard grunted and staggered back against the cell bars. He grabbed a bar and steadied himself.

Blood dripped from the guard's split lip. He cursed in Spanish as he touched his jaw and licked the blood away. With his thumb, he motioned at the other guard, who stood lookout at the bars. Then he moved to the center of the cell.

"That was a big mistake, my friend." He waved his index finger at the prisoner. "You *norteamericanos*, you never understand how things work down here."

The guard unclipped his baton from his duty belt. He

rolled up his shirtsleeves, revealing the prominent tattoo of a black scorpion on his forearm.

"Now you get a lesson."

Pueblo de Pescado, Mexico

THE MURDER OF BLACK CROWS, ITS AGITATED *"CAW-CAW"* calls echoing back and forth in annoying concert, circled slowly in the burnt-orange sky of sunset.

Michael Quinn focused his binoculars until he could see the birds' feathers fluttering in the wind. Other than the noise of the birds, silence surrounded him.

The rubbish-strewn room of the abandoned hotel was a good spot for recon, even with its musty stench and late-afternoon heat. The hotel sat in a deserted area of vacant, crumbling old buildings, and the top-floor room's open window gave him a panoramic view.

Why had the word "murder" been assigned to describe such an innocuous group of birds? Yes, these crows were on the hunt, looking for their dinner, and hunting involved killing. But crows were probably always on the hunt. As were all animals. As were all living things.

He tilted the binoculars down and scanned the birds' hunting ground.

The sprawling compound of the *Prisión Federal Norte Baja* would make for a reliable source of nourishment. Scraps of bread or meat always littered the grimy asphalt prison yards. And the end of the day, when the outdoor areas were largely empty, was a good time to go foraging for food.

A half-dozen crows broke away from the rest, swooping down toward a trashcan topped by a ripped paper bag that held the remnants of someone's meal.

"This is Spartan 33. Take the bird solo." Quinn spoke into the microphone of his earpiece. He leaned forward in his chair and tightened his grip on the binoculars.

Another crow broke away from the rest. It flapped its wings and flew in a smooth downward arc toward the trashcan. In the hazy sunset, the solitary crow looked very much like the others.

But this crow's eyes were camera lenses, its wings were black carbon fiber, its heartbeat electronic impulses.

Quinn tapped an icon on the tablet computer next to him and entered the encryption code. The app opened to reveal the drone's video feed—a high-resolution aerial view of the prison grounds. The trashcan loomed large on the screen as the drone dove down.

"Got the feed." Quinn used his thumb and finger to adjust the tablet image. "Bring the bird back up and over the target cell."

The drone flapped its wings and flew away from the trashcan, toward a squalid, one-story concrete building in a corner of the compound. It circled over a section of the flat rooftop.

"That entire building is solitary." The voice of Will, Quinn's field supervisor, crackled in his earpiece. "Your man's cell is directly under the bird. Third cell in from that side entrance with the dirt courtyard."

"Bring the bird up over the entire compound. Let's see what we're dealing with."

The drone flew back up to join the circling crows, then leveled out and began a long, lazy loop around the perimeter of the prison complex.

Quinn put down the binoculars and picked up the tablet, scrutinizing the aerial view through the bird's eyes.

The notorious maximum-security *Prisión Federal*, known by locals as the *guarida del diablo*—the devil's lair—looked like it did in the photographs: a compound of dingy gray buildings, interspersed with asphalt yards and a parking lot. A fifteen-foot concrete wall topped with barbed wire and alarm horns at regular intervals surrounded the prison.

Here and there, chips and cracks and graffiti marred the buildings' thick concrete walls. The buildings looked at least fifty years old and like they hadn't been cleaned since.

Behind a steel sliding entry door built into the concrete wall, eight black-clad guards holding rifles stood around or inside the guardhouse. Four guards with rifles occupied each of the watchtowers, the towers themselves concrete fortresses wrapped in double layers of barbed wire. Other guards, carrying shotguns and wearing holstered sidearms on their hips, roamed the grounds in pairs.

"Will, you want me to get this guy out of there with zero collateral damage?"

"That's the goal."

"What did you have in mind? We can't helo in at night and fast-rope down to the roof. With the engine roar, they'd be all over us. An operation like this would require fifteen, maybe twenty men. We'd have to hike in from a couple of miles away. Stage a predawn raid."

"Michael, relations with Mexico are shaky enough now. We can't risk multiple casualties. And with a worst-case scenario, we can't risk having a group of American special ops forces captured assaulting a Mexican prison. It would be a nightmare of an international incident."

Will paused, then continued. "We need someone who's totally off the books and who can get this done. That means you, my friend, flying solo. And soon. You know the high value of this asset. What you don't know is how precarious his situation is."

Quinn tapped another icon on his tablet. The screen shifted to a color photograph of a brown-haired American soldier, dressed in camouflage clothes and holding a rifle. He looked to be in his mid-twenties.

It was a bright sunny day, and the man stood in front of a background of craggy brown mountains that Quinn guessed to be Afghanistan. The man stood about six foot three, broad-shouldered and bearded, and gazed stoically at the camera. Quinn recognized him immediately.

"I've heard of Bobby Devereaux. One of the best snipers in the SEALs. What else can you tell me?"

"You already know the *Escorpiones* drug cartel has been spreading aggressively into California and Texas. They've even taken over some border towns on the Mexico side. Intel uncovered a plot to kidnap Americans for ransom. They're going to start by beheading a couple of Americans, just to let us know they're serious. Then they'll settle into the kidnap-ransom routine as a long-term business plan. It's worked well for them elsewhere."

Will's voice lowered. "The DEA and Homeland Security were getting nowhere. Covert action was needed. The decision was made to send in Devereaux to take out the *Escorpiones'* head guy."

"That's showing some stones."

"It would have sent the *Escorpiones* the message to not mess with the U.S. And, with a little creative assistance from us, it also would have ignited a turf war with a rival gang."

Quinn looked at the photo of the soldier. "From what I've heard about Devereaux, he likes to work alone. How was he going to get close to the target?"

"We have an informant inside the *Escorpiones*. He was going to tip us off as to the right time and place. Remember, Devereaux has taken out hostiles from up to a mile away. The opportunity would have arisen for a clean shot. You were right about him insisting on going alone. He made it across the border okay, just him in his pickup truck."

"What went wrong?"

"Mexican police pulled him over. They said he was speeding, which was a crock. It was a shakedown, of course. But Devereaux hadn't brought enough cash to satisfy them. So they searched his truck. They found the hidden compartment in his truck bed, and there was his sniper rifle, a high-powered scope, and boxes of ammo."

Will sighed. "That did it. The Mexican authorities went ballistic when they saw the sniper gear. Devereaux's been locked up in solitary for over two months now, still waiting for a hearing."

"Do the Mexicans know who he is?"

"His false ID is holding up so far. They didn't for a second buy his story about going out target shooting and making a wrong turn into Mexico, but they don't know who he really is. That's the only reason he's still alive."

Will's voice was somber. "But it's only a matter of time—days, maybe—until they find out. And any way it goes down, it's bad. If the Mexican government finds out who he is, then we're in the extremely awkward position of having sent an American assassin into a foreign country. Devereaux will get life in a Mexican hellhole.

"And if it's the *Escorpiones* that find out who he is—and for all we know, they run that damn prison—then he'll simply disappear. And some cold morning, his head will turn up on a Tijuana street corner."

Quinn cursed. His tightening gut always told him when a situation had no good options.

He tapped the tablet screen, and the picture changed back to the video feed from the drone. "Will, bring that bird up higher. I want to see what's around this prison."

The drone flapped its wings and soared high above the crows, then it curved into a long, graceful arc. Quinn studied the aerial view on his tablet screen.

Like many prisons, the *Prisión Federal Norte Baja* was located outside of town, in a barren area where no one lived or would ever want to live. On each side of the prison walls lay a football-field-sized chunk of land with nothing but dirt and rocks.

Past the land stood a few industrial plants that, from their appearance, were so polluting and repulsive that they too, along with the prison, had been exiled to the badlands.

On one side of the prison, an industrial complex of four humble, tin-roofed buildings formed a square. In the center of the square lay a large pile of animal bones and carrion. Quinn recognized horse and cow ribcages sticking up in the air. The place was a rendering plant.

On the other side of the prison stood a larger, more modern-looking industrial plant. A maze of large pipes connected steel cylindrical tanks and concrete buildings, interspersed with huge smokestacks. The tanker trucks in the parking lot confirmed it was some sort of chemical plant. The brightly colored pictures of produce on the sides of the trucks indicated a food-processing business.

The businesses farther out were more of the same—enterprises that no one wanted around. A decrepit complex of wood buildings with large tubs of dirty liquids and piles of animal hides lying on the ground—a tannery. A large lot that looked like a sea of old metal glinting in the sun, interspersed with patches of rust and piles of dirty tires—a wrecking yard.

Chain link fences topped with barbed wire surrounded all of the businesses. They all undoubtedly had their own alarm systems. Above them, the concentration of multiple pollutants had turned the sky into a permanent brown haze that shrouded everything in gloom.

This entire area was the *guarida del diablo*.

"Will, there's got to be another way. Get the State Department involved, call a meeting, exert some diplomatic pressure."

"We already have." The frustration was evident in Will's voice. "And we're getting stonewalled. Devereaux's sniper gear must've set off alarms that went to the top of the Mexican government."

"Then go to the bottom. Money changes hands. The charges are dropped. Devereaux is quietly escorted out in the middle of the night."

"We tried that in the very beginning." Will's voice rose. "We got squat. This stone wall is solid from the bottom to the top."

"Will, you've got to have a Plan B."

"We do, Michael." Will took a breath and lowered his voice. "Our Plan B is you."

Washington, D.C.

"LET ME ASSURE YOU ONCE AGAIN, MR. JENKINS."

The man from the office of the Mexican SRE, the *Secretaria de Relaciones Exteriores,* spoke with the practiced patience of a diplomat. "The American's rights as a foreign national are being completely respected. He will have his right to due process. He will have a fair hearing."

The Mexican official sipped from his glass of ice water, then placed his brown hands on the mahogany conference table next to his laptop. His broad shoulders filled out his well-cut, navy pin-stripe suit, and his jet-black hair glistened in the fluorescent light of the drop ceiling. The bronze skin of his face was unlined for someone in early middle age, and he looked cool and comfortable in the air-conditioned room.

"And my country appreciates that, Mr. Hernandez." Jenkins kept his voice equally modulated.

He glanced down at his pale hands. In comparison to the skin of Mr. Hernandez, they looked the color of alabaster, and his pale, bald head probably looked like a cue ball in the fluorescent lights.

An incident like this could easily spiral out of control. His job was to do everything in his power to ensure it did not.

Glancing at his laptop, he resisted the urge to drum his fingers on the conference table. "What we are asking for is your cooperation in the expedition of this matter, so that the American can be released in a timely fashion and return home to the United States."

The Mexican official raised his hands off of the table and faced his palms toward Jenkins. "Let me be clear, Mr. Jenkins. We will do what we can to help. We can speak again to the office of the Mexican Attorney General. We can speak again to the office of the Governor of Baja California. We can ask them to do what they can to facilitate the processes of the *burocracia.*

"But what we cannot do—" The raised palms moved slightly forward in emphasis. "—is in any way circumvent our laws. This American was caught in our country with—" Hernandez glanced at his laptop screen. "—a Desert Tactical SRS 'bullpup' rifle, a suppressor, a high-powered Leupold riflescope, and considerable quantities of Lapua .338 match-grade ammunition. In our country, the possession alone of such things is a very serious offense, a federal offense. One that may result in years in prison.

"And this American, his past, or lack thereof, it seems to

raise questions. It is correct, as you pointed out, that he has no criminal record. It is also correct that there is not much record of anything about this man, other than employment as an insurance claims processor. Such a man has never served in the military, but carries around the equipment of a trained soldier?

"You know that in our country, as in your country, ignorance of the law is no excuse. We are a democracy, a nation of laws, like your country. And we must uphold our laws. Surely you have no reason to think otherwise?" The Mexican official laid his palms back on the table and leaned back in his chair.

"Of course not, Mr. Hernandez." Jenkins forced a reassuring smile and, replicating his counterpart's body language, sat back in his chair.

Oh, I don't know why we would think otherwise, Jenkins thought. *Perhaps because huge chunks of your country are a frigging lawless narco-state, run by warring drug cartels that torture and murder at will?*

He picked up his glass of ice water and drank, allowing himself a few extra seconds to confirm what he had already decided, that it was time to bring in the big guns. The back of his shirt collar was damp with sweat. As he put the glass down, he put the smile back on his face.

"We at the State Department fully understand, Mr. Hernandez. You must work within your own legal system. We respect that." Jenkins cleared his throat. *Careful now.* "It's just that we do not want this to escalate into any kind of diplomatic conflict. Conflict that could have political ramifications with regard to the tariffs currently under renegotiation. Conflict that could decrease popular support for the substantial aid our country continues to provide to your country."

Better stop there. He kept the smile on his face and waited.

For a moment, Hernandez's dark eyes glittered with what may have been anger. Then the moment passed, and the eyes showed only resignation, boredom at having to be there when there were so many more important matters to be handled elsewhere.

He spoke with a quiet finality. "I have my superiors to answer to, as do you, Mr. Jenkins. And we wish to do nothing to endanger your government's very generous support." The official closed his laptop and stood, pushing back his chair. "You must now excuse me. I have another appointment for which I am behind schedule." He placed the laptop in his briefcase.

"When can we meet again?" Jenkins felt the cold sweat against the back of his neck.

"When we have something new to discuss." Hernandez turned and opened the door to the hallway. He stopped in the doorway and turned back. "I mean to say, when we have made progress on this matter. Perhaps when this American has his court hearing? That should happen soon. No more than a month or two from now."

He turned and walked out of the room.

Jenkins sat back in his chair and sighed. He had so much more on his plate than this case. But he had to do whatever he could. The cell phone in his inside coat pocket vibrated. He removed it and looked at the screen.

Status? read the encrypted text.

He tapped the keys, his reply not bothering with diplomatic niceties.

Status is we are still being jerked around. Zero. Nada. If you have Plan B, recommend you pull trigger.

Three days later
La Encantada Hotel
Pueblo de Pescado, Mexico

WITH ANY OPERATION, THE WAITING WAS THE HARDEST part.

The best ops were simple and quick. Simple, because things always changed. Quick, because each individual step had been drilled into muscle memory. Sketch it out, review carefully once or twice, and then fifteen minutes later get it done.

The operation Quinn was about to execute met none of those criteria.

At his corner table in the hotel bar, Quinn stared at the bottle of Negra Modelo he was pretending to drink. Though he'd been up all night, the pills he'd taken at dawn still had him wired. He absent-mindedly scratched the day-old stubble on his chin.

In his mind, he checked and rechecked his gear again, then he ran through the operation for what seemed like the hundredth time. He couldn't escape the fact that this plan could go wrong in countless ways.

With hours to kill before an operation, time wasn't his friend. His mind dreamt up unrealistic contingencies. Bizarre worst-case scenarios, all of them just possible enough to rattle him but still extremely unlikely, lurked in the corners of his mind like ghosts.

He forced his eyes away from the beer and glanced around the room. The hotel bar was getting crowded as late Friday afternoon segued into the evening mix of tourists and locals.

This place was the right spot for killing time. Large and stylish enough to be popular. Yet casual enough for him in his T-shirt, Crye pants, and hiking boots to blend in as just another weekend warrior, down in Mexico to have a little fun in the desert.

The happy-hour buzz of conversation faded into the background as his gaze shifted to the window behind the bar. From his corner table, he could see the alley behind the hotel and the stained, discarded blanket hanging off the dumpster and fully covering his motorcycle.

What had Quinn heard about this Bobby Devereaux? Not much.

Country boy. Quiet, polite. Kept to himself.

What sort of miserable cell was Devereaux stuck in? The battles between the drug cartels kept getting worse. Would Mexico someday collapse into the equivalent of a Somalia, a failed state run by warlords?

"Excuse me, *señor*."

A whiff of spicy perfume accompanied the feminine voice. From behind him, his cocktail waitress placed a chilled bottle of Negra Modelo on his table.

"I brought you a new *cerveza* since —ah, you have scarcely touched the first one. I will take this one back?"

"It's okay, *señorita*. You can leave the new bottle and take the old. I like my beer cold." Quinn looked down at his table and didn't say anything more. He hadn't paid any attention to her when he had ordered his drink, and he wasn't going to start now. It was important to stay anonymous.

"Of course, *señor*." The waitress leaned in and picked up the old bottle. As she did so the bar rag on her drink tray slipped off and fell forward, onto the floor underneath Quinn's table. "*Lo siento.*"

Before Quinn could react, the waitress stepped forward and bent over next to the table to pick up the rag. As she did, her thigh bumped the table, and the ends of her long mane of coal-black hair spilled over onto Quinn's forearm.

His skin tingled at the touch, and for a second, he just stared at the shiny luster of the beautiful black hair resting on his forearm. Her spicy perfume was stronger and had a touch of some kind of exotic fruit.

Her torso was only inches to the left of his face. The waitress grunted as she stretched under the table to reach the rag, which had landed close to the wall. As she bent over farther, her short, black pleated skirt fell forward, enough to reveal the beautiful bronze curves of her legs.

Ten thousand years ago, Quinn's primitive male ancestor simply would have reached over and grabbed hold of her. Such a woman would be a prize possession, one to keep for an extended period of time.

The primitive urge pulled every bit as strongly now, but the bonds of civilization restrained Quinn, and he politely averted his gaze. He looked down, but that was of little help, as he saw golden calf muscles bulging from feet atop black stiletto-heeled shoes.

And, hey, those long legs went all the way down to the

ground, didn't they? Only athletes had legs like that. Maybe she was a runner. Or a soccer player. Or—

"Are you a dancer?" Quinn sat back in his chair, pushing its back against the wall, providing a little more gentlemanly space between the two of them. He'd changed his mind about conversation. A little idle chitchat would kill time and help him blend in with the bar crowd.

"Oh!" The waitress stood up straight, realizing what had happened. Embarrassed at her exposure, she straightened her skirt and top, adjusting everything back in place while Quinn gazed at his beer.

"I am a dancer." She tossed her mane of hair over one shoulder and looked warily at Quinn. "Why?"

"Because you're in such great shape." He gave her a reassuring smile. "Only dancers and athletes stay so fit. And your poise is that of a dancer."

Her body language relaxed. "I dance here in the hotel showroom." She gave him an appraising glance, then a note of pride filled her voice. "I am in the weekend revue. You would like to come see the show, maybe?"

"I'd love to, but I'm leaving tonight." Quinn glanced at his watch. He had more time to kill. "I'd like to hear more about your dancing, though. I imagine you're quite passionate about it."

She looked around the room and, deciding she had time to talk, leaned against the table. "It is only part-time. Two nights a week. A nice little show for the *turistas*. It has a little of everything—salsa, tango, samba. Waiting tables, that is what pays my bills. But you are right, *señor*. Someday I hope to make it my career. My dream is to go to New York and, I think you say, go for it?"

"I don't know anything about dance, but I imagine that's the place."

"Ah!" The brown eyes flashed. "To see Broadway, to audition for the shows. And to audition for the great schools, like Ailey, Juilliard. I took ballet as a child, so maybe I get in. Already I reach the limit of what I can do here in this small town. I would be happy to be in any show in New York."

"Let me know when you're there, and I'll come watch you dance." Quinn extended his hand. "I'm Michael."

"Gabriella." She clasped his hand.

Their hands stayed clasped a bit longer than normal for an introduction. As Quinn continued to make small talk with her, he settled back in his chair and took her in.

She was tall, maybe five-foot-eight. About twenty, twenty-one. Her thick black hair hung straight down almost to her waist. Her figure made Quinn's heart pound. And her face, while a bit angular for some men, had a natural look he found appealing.

She was, as beautiful Mexican women often are, an ethnic mix. *Mestizo*—was that still the word? Olive skin, a narrow European-looking nose, full lips—those came from the Spanish empire, from some fair-skinned *conquistador* marrying a native girl long ago. But her high cheekbones, her square jawline, and, most of all, the fiery glint in her dark-almond eyes—those were Aztec.

Her shortie top left her slim waist exposed, and her pleated black skirt barely reached the top of her muscular thighs. In bed, this woman would be an animal. Quinn was wondering if he could reach both hands around her waist when he realized she was asking him a question.

"… should go check my other tables. Where are you from? Maybe I will see you around."

"California. Not too far." What to say next? "We could get together when you make that trip to New York," he finished lamely.

At the remark, her countenance fell. Had he unwittingly struck a nerve?

"That is still a dream. I am just sort of getting by, I think you say? You know, making just enough to pay my bills. I am embarrassed to say this, but I have never been to the United States. I have never even been outside Mexico. So, my new friend Michael, yes, New York. Someday."

"You're on your own, then?"

"For a long time."

"Same here. I like the freedom. But I know what you mean. It's not always the easiest path to where you want to go."

She hesitated, then she leaned down and in. Her hair brushed his arm again as her face moved close. Her dark brown eyes searched his.

"Do you ever feel sort of trapped? That life, it is okay, you know, but that you are just on a, I think you call it, a treadmill. Do you ever feel like you want to, you know, escape? Just break out?"

She stood up and tilted her head back, awaiting his reply with a kind of dignity that came from pouring out her heart. When he gave no reply, she turned sideways, legs slightly apart as if, now that she had opened up, she was daring him to hurry up and make his evasive, non-committal, conversation-ending reply so she could walk away and go back to work.

Her honesty reflected a vitality that embraced life. And her body language said she'd just thrown down some sort of gauntlet. Yes, that was it. She had just offered him a smoldering, sexual *challenge.*

"I know exactly what you mean, Gabriella." Quinn grabbed a cocktail napkin and wrote down the number of his disposable cell phone. The number would no longer exist after tonight, and thus it wouldn't compromise his mission. "Here's my cell number. I'm also writing down the name of the hotel where I'm staying. It's about two hours north of here, not far from the border.

"I'm busy with work this evening but should be back by midnight. If you'd like to break out of here, text me after midnight from the bar at my hotel, and I'll meet you there. After tonight, I've got a few days off. And New York is only a five-hour flight away."

Gabriella raised her eyebrows. Then, with a what-do-I-have-to-lose shrug, she picked up the cocktail napkin and tucked it into her skirt pocket.

She turned away, about to say goodbye, when a thunderous *boom* sounded in the distance.

Heads perked up all around the bar as glassware rattled on shelves, and the bottle of beer on Quinn's table vibrated. The noisy buzz of the crowd faded away.

"What was that?" asked Gabriella.

WASHINGTON, D.C.

The Mexican official from the *Secretaria de Relaciones Exteriores* no longer looked cool and comfortable. His brow furrowed as he leaned forward in his chair, and he let out an exasperated sigh as he turned a page of the thick document lying on the conference table.

"This document, Mr. Jenkins, it could have been sent to us digitally. We could have discussed it over the phone. Why did your colleagues at the Department of State insist that it be reviewed in a face-to-face meeting?"

"For security reasons, Mr. Hernandez. That's all we're able to say." Jenkins put a polite smile on his face. "I'm sorry for the inconvenience. Shall we move on to the next page? I believe it is number 138."

Hernandez frowned. "Why is it necessary to review each page? Why not an executive summary? So far I see nothing new here. No new facts at all regarding this American."

"It was at the request of members of Congress, sir," Jenkins said. "Some representatives have introduced legislation that would suspend all foreign aid to your country until there has been marked improvement in the issues of crime and border security. These issues are so serious that they now impact the United States. We do appreciate your cooperation."

Hernandez muttered under his breath, then glanced at the flashing blue screen of his vibrating cell phone. He answered the phone curtly and spoke commandingly in rapid Spanish

In mid-sentence, he stopped talking and sat upright as he listened. His demeanor changed to that of a man now taking orders. His eyes widened as he tapped keys on his laptop and looked at the screen.

Jenkins could also see the laptop screen from where he was sitting. The full screen showed a live, breaking-news broadcast from a Mexican television station.

Most of the screen showed helicopter footage of a huge fire with yellow-orange flames leaping high in the air and billowing clouds of reddish-brown smoke. The video alternated with helicopter footage of an entirely different scene, one of Mexican citizens evacuating a small town.

The video also showed the panicked citizenry clogging the streets as they fled by car and truck, by bicycle, and by foot, trying to escape the billowing clouds in the sky above them. A few Mexican police cars sped about, their flashing red and blue lights rendering some semblance of order to the chaos.

In the lower right-hand corner of the screen, a box showed an attractive dark-haired female news anchor, but the laptop sound was turned off. At the bottom of the screen, a scroll with bold, white capital letters summarized the breaking news, and Jenkins managed to translate the scrolling Spanish sentence fragments.

MASSIVE EXPLOSION AT CHEMICAL FOOD-PROCESSING PLANT ... JUST OUTSIDE TOWN OF PUEBLO DE PESCADO ... LARGE QUANTITIES OF NITRIC ACID ACCIDENTALLY POURED INTO TANKS CONTAINING SODIUM HYDROXIDE ... CHEMICAL REACTION PRODUCED TOXIC GASES WHICH ARE EXTREMELY DANGEROUS IF ANY CONTACT WITH THE HUMAN BODY ... PLANT SENSOR SYSTEM DETECTED EXPLOSION, SENT ALARM SIGNAL ORDERING EVACUATION ... LARGE CLOUDS OF GASES SPREAD RAPIDLY BY WINDS ... ALL EMPLOYEES OF ADJACENT FACILITIES, INCLUDING PRISIÓN FEDERAL, ORDERED TO

IMMEDIATELY EVACUATE VICINITY ... RISK ZONE EXTENDED
TO INCLUDE TOWN OF PUEBLO DE PESCADO ... SPECIALIST
TEAMS WITH HAZMAT SUITS EXPECTED TO ARRIVE BY LATE
EVENING...

"*Madre de Dios*," Hernandez spoke softly as he stared at the screen.

Jenkins raised his eyebrows in an expression of polite concern. "Is something wrong?"

Pueblo de Pescado, Mexico

QUINN'S 500CC DIRT BIKE SHOT DOWN THE ALLEY, THEN slowed as it turned onto the boulevard.

The street was already a gridlock of cars and trucks, and a chorus of car horns and angry yells filled the smoky air.

But Quinn had expected this. He flicked the bike onto the sidewalk.

He snaked around startled pedestrians, guiding the bike through whatever pockets of space opened up in front of him, alternating between the street curbside and the sidewalk. Word of the evacuation had spread quickly, and people spilled out from buildings and stores.

He made his way through city blocks, amid a blur of jabbering faces, then turned into an alley he'd memorized as part of his escape route. The alley was blessedly empty and led him to a series of quiet side streets. A final turn, and then he hit the highway leading to the *Prisión*.

Now he was ahead of the fleeing populace, and traffic on the highway was light. The bike whined as he pushed it to seventy, then eighty. The turnoff for the prison loomed on his right. He slowed for the curving exit ramp then brought the bike onto the long driveway that led only to the prison.

Ahead of him, the entrance came into view. The text he'd received confirmed that the gate was jammed open and the yards and watchtowers were empty. All of the guards and employees had fled immediately upon hearing the evacuation order, leaving the prisoners behind.

He slowed the bike to a crawl and rode through the entrance, glancing at his holstered HK 9mm.

With the prison adjacent to the chemical plant, smoke billowed everywhere, several times thicker than in town. A reddish-brown haze hung to the ground, so dense it partially obscured the buildings.

The compound was now a fire-and-brimstone hell, the *guarida del diablo*. The dimmed sun turned the day into a sulfurous twilight with everything covered in soot. The alarm horns had finished, and only the dull rumble of the prisoners trapped in the cells sounded from within, their shouting muffled by thick concrete walls.

Quinn guided the bike through the haze to the side entrance of the solitary building. He dismounted, chained the bike to one of the bars on the window next to the entry door, and clipped the key ring to his belt.

The smoke stung his eyes and irritated his lungs. He drew his 9mm and approached the open entry door from the side to make sure it was clear. As he entered the building, the rumble of the prisoners increased to a roar.

The one-story building stank of urine and vomit, and the prisoners reached through the bars and shouted for help. Quinn ignored them and jogged down to the third cell on his right.

Something was wrong.

The man in the filthy cell didn't look like the Devereaux in the photograph. The gaunt, pale-skinned figure in a dirty T-shirt and khakis, sitting forlornly on the bunk, resembled a picture from a concentration camp. His eyes had a hollow, deep-set stare.

Quinn examined the facial features. "Bobby Devereaux?"

"No, sir. I'm—hold on." The man stood and moved forward as far as the ankle chains padlocked to his bunk would allow. "Who the hell are you?"

"What's your birthday, Devereaux?" The facial structure and eye color matched, but Quinn needed to be sure.

"November twelfth."

"Good answer. And your mother's maiden name?"

"Long. You special ops?"

"Affirmative, Devereaux. Here to get you out. Stand back. I'm going to use a lock-popper."

The chains clanked as Devereaux retreated to the rear corner of his bunk.

Quinn attached a foot-long adhesive strip to the cell door lock, then he stepped back. Both men turned their heads away, and with a *bang*, the breaching charge blew the door open.

"What the hell's goin' on outside?" Devereaux's words tumbled out. "Everyone's yellin' 'bout some explosion at the chemical plant next door. Sayin' that the clouds of toxic smoke

241

floatin' over are gonna kill us all, that the goddam coward guards left us here to die."

"Hold up your wrists." Quinn pulled a pair of bolt-cutters out of his backpack and cut away Devereaux's handcuffs. "The smoke clouds are all a fake. A ruse to get you out of here. Tell you more later." He glanced at the bruises and welts on the prisoner's face and arms, then knelt down and cut away the ankle chains. "Can you walk?"

"I'll run like a damn jackrabbit to get outta here."

"Follow me."

Quinn jogged back toward the open doorway. So far, so good. He had his hands on the key ring on his belt and had just passed from the dark building's doorway into the outdoors when an arm grabbed him around the neck and shoved him forward.

He stumbled on the porch step and fell. As he brought his arms up to break his fall, he saw the steel blade of a shiv coming up at him, going for his throat.

He grabbed the man's knife hand with both hands and twisted hard to the right, forcing the man to fall down with him or have his wrist broken.

Both men toppled to the dirt. The man was choking him with the arm around his neck, but Quinn kept a tight grip on the man's knife hand and twisted it further until the wrist broke with an audible *snap*.

The man screamed and let go of the knife. Quinn delivered a sharp elbow jab to the man's throat, and the scream became choking sounds.

Quinn rolled over in the dirt until he was clear. His attacker, a shirtless Mexican prisoner with an upper body covered in gang tattoos, writhed in the dirt, his usable hand on his throat.

A few yards away, Devereaux scuffled in the dirt with another prisoner, also a tattooed gangbanger.

Quinn sprang to his feet and drew his 9mm, looking for a clean shot.

The prisoner saw the gun trained on him, put Devereaux in a chokehold, and wrenched him to his feet in front of him, blocking Quinn's shot. The gangbanger brought his other arm up and held the point of his shiv blade against Devereaux's throat. Devereaux froze, and the prisoner stepped back, facing off against Quinn.

"*Las llaves! Ahora!*" The prisoner threatened with a slicing motion across Devereaux's throat.

"*Sí, sí, no problema.*" Quinn grabbed his key ring and, moving slowly and deliberately, unclipped it from his belt.

Devereaux stood still, the knifepoint pressed tight against his throat. He made eye contact with Quinn then glanced at both of his hands.

Devereaux's left hand held a fistful of dirt, and his right forearm had moved up until it was behind, but not touching, the forearm of the man's knife hand. Quinn looked back at Devereaux and nodded.

"*Sí, sí, amigo.* You can have the motorcycle keys." Quinn held out the key ring and jangled the keys. "See? Here they are. You can have the keys right *now.*"

He tossed the keys directly at the gangbanger's face.

At the same time, Devereaux shoved the man's knife arm forward and rubbed his fistful of dirt in the man's eyes. The man yelled as Devereaux dropped down and rolled away.

Quinn fired two rounds into the gangbanger's bare chest and another into his head. The man crumpled to the ground, gurgling. Quinn walked over and fired another round into the head. The man stopped making noise and lay still.

The gangbanger with the broken wrist had pushed himself up on one arm, crawling toward the dead man's knife. Quinn turned and fired three quick rounds. The gangbanger rolled onto his back and lay there motionless, blood streaking his face.

Quinn picked up the key ring, unchained the bike, straddled it, and fired it up. Devereaux climbed on the rear seat.

"Hold on," Quinn shouted over the whine of the engine. He pointed to dark shapes moving in the haze around other buildings. Prisoners were pouring out of the building exits. "We're not outta here yet. The way out's going to get busy."

He pulled the bike out of the courtyard and rounded the corner of the solitary building, heading toward the entrance. Ahead of him, the once-empty prison yards now looked like a village of the damned.

Ghostly shapes everywhere appeared and then disappeared into the thick smoke as panicked prisoners fled in all directions. Screams and shrieks echoed off the abandoned buildings. Quinn threaded the bike around the shadowy shapes, slowing when he had to, speeding up whenever he hit a patch of empty asphalt.

A bottle smashed to the ground in front of them, showering them in shards of glass, and Quinn swerved hard to the left. The tires screeched in protest.

A prisoner grabbed Devereaux's leg, trying to knock them over. Devereaux kicked out, but the man held on and the bike wobbled. Quinn aimed the bike at one of the concrete build-ings and twisted the accelerator.

The bike shot forward, dragging the prisoner along in the dirt. As he reached the wall, Quinn slowed and turned the bike so that it was parallel to the building, pinning the pris-oner against the concrete wall, then gunned the bike again. The man screamed as the rough concrete tore off skin and clothing.

Devereaux kicked out again. This time the man let go and rolled away in the dirt behind them.

Now the entrance was visible ahead. Prisoners ran at them from all sides, trying to cut them off. Quinn jerked the bike right, left, right, inches beyond a blur of grasping hands and shouting faces.

The bike engine screamed as they shot through the open gate and onto the long driveway. Bottles crashed into the asphalt behind them, and the yells of the prisoners faded into the background.

At the highway, Quinn slowed and turned left, away from town. The road ahead looked empty. The citizens of Pueblo de Pescado had fled in the other direction, toward the next closest city.

Now for the homestretch. Quinn twisted the throttle, and the bike tore down the blacktop. The desert became an endless blur, and ahead of them the sun diminished to a copper-colored streak on the horizon.

They rode in silence as stars appeared in the darkening sky. The heat of the day gave way to shadowy twilight. The only sounds were the whine of the engine and the roar of the wind.

By the time Quinn pulled over and turned off the highway

into the desert, night had fallen. In the darkness, he kept the bike's speed to twenty, using the headlight to guide the bike over undulating sand hills punctuated by mesquite and creosote. About a half-hour in he stopped, checked the GPS on his cell phone, and killed the engine.

"Okay, Bobby, here's where we dismount and stretch our legs. We're almost home." As he walked, he tapped the keys on his phone and put it on speaker. "This is Spartan 33, Atlas 11 come in."

"Go ahead, Spartan 33," crackled a voice.

"Atlas 11, I have Bulls-eye in position. Repeat, have Bulls-eye in position."

"Spartan 33, copy. We are ten minutes out. Mark position to identify."

Quinn removed a rectangular object the size of a flashlight from his backpack, walked several yards out, and placed it on a level patch of sand with its lens facing up.

"Atlas 11, this is Spartan 33. Position marked by IR strobe. Ready for extract."

"Spartan 33, copy. On our way."

Devereaux watched. "A helo?"

Quinn pointed. "From behind those hills."

Devereaux gave a long sigh of relief. He extended his hand. "I don't believe I got your name."

"Michael Quinn." They shook hands.

"That was a hell of a stunt you pulled off back there, Michael. What'd you rig up at that plant? Smoke bombs?"

"In large quantities, so the winds would spread the smoke. For the explosion, I used C4 to blow up an empty warehouse. Accelerant for the fire."

"And that alarm?"

"Cyberintel hacked the plant's computer system to set off the toxic-gas alarm and evacuation order. By now the hazmat teams are probably at the plant, surprised to find there were never toxic gases of any kind."

"Appreciate you savin' my ass. Things looked a bit grim back there." He coughed—a racking cough that shook his upper body—and spat in the sand.

Quinn removed two water bottles from the bike's saddlebag and handed one to Devereaux. He had liked the man instinctively. "The SEALs weren't about to let anything happen to one of their best men. You've been through quite a bit, Bobby. Any plans for when you get home?"

Devereaux took a long drink from the bottle and looked out at the stars. His gaunt face was pensive.

"Had plenty of time to think 'bout that." He took another drink. "Got a girl back home. Been goin' together three years now. Cute little thing. A runner. I can see her bouncing blonde ponytail now. Gotta good job, too, a physical therapist.

"She's been patient, waitin' for me. And I been puttin' her off, 'cause of my work, me being gone so much. You know how it is.

"Lotta guys lose their girlfriends, even their wives, 'cause of that. It seems like you're overseas most all the time, and then, even when you're back home, in your mind you're still gone.

"That ain't gonna happen to me. Two months wastin' away in that hellhole of a cell taught me that you never know when your own number's gonna come up. We're only here for a while, y'know?"

Devereaux finished the last of his water and gazed at something far away.

"So, when I get home I'm gonna grab this girl and pop the question. And if she'll have me, I ain't never lettin' her go."

The men stood in silence. The nighttime desert was a different world from the smoky inferno of the day. The bright moon cast its luminescence across endless rippled sand. Stars glittered quietly against a jet-black sky.

Devereaux glanced at Quinn. "What about you? You got someone special?"

Before Quinn could reply, a rhythmic thumping noise sliced through the air, and the men searched the sky.

Thunderous rotor beats echoed as the dark silhouette of the Blackhawk helicopter rose up from behind the hills. Quinn put on his night-vision goggles and pointed Devereaux to where the silhouette of the helicopter blotted out a patch of stars.

The chopper flew toward them, then it hovered over a flat stretch of desert as it descended. The rotor wash kicked up a brief whirling sandstorm as the helo landed.

Quinn motioned for Devereaux to climb back on the bike. He kept it in first gear as he eased it over to the waiting Blackhawk. When they closed to within a few yards, the helo's passenger door opened.

He stopped the bike and turned to Devereaux. "The pilots will take over from here. They'll ID you to make sure who you are. Then the chopper will take you to a hospital in Camp Pendleton. They'll make sure you're okay, debrief you, get some food in you, and then get you home."

"You ain't comin'?" Devereaux looked surprised as he dismounted.

"Bobby, after what went down today, I can't be seen within a hundred miles of you. But I've got a feeling our paths will cross again."

"I hope so. Looks like things ain't dull when you're around."

Quinn's disposable cell phone beeped in his back pocket. He fished the phone out and glanced at the flashing blue screen. A simple text message.

I am here. Gabriella.

"And my day's not quite over." Quinn tapped the keys and sent his reply. "I've got one more stop to make tonight."

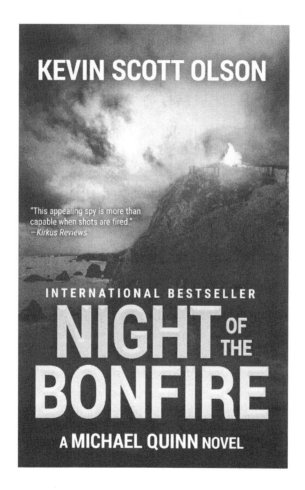

For more works by the author, please visit

WWW.KEVINSCOTTOLSON.COM